BLUE FATE 2
BUYOUT

CASS TELL

BLUE FATE 2
BUYOUT

A novella from the Blue Fate series

destinēe

Buyout (Blue Fate 2)
by Cass Tell

Copyright © 2013 Destinée Media

Cover concept by Per-Ole Lind

Published by Destinée Media
www.destineemedia.com
info@destineemedia.com

ISBN 978-0-9832768-7-6

CHAPTER 1

The private detective waited for the person to emerge from the building. He had been there three hours, sitting stationary in his light blue Ford. It didn't matter. Each hour was billable and the more the clock ticked the more he was paid.

He liked to think of the person as his 'target', but there was no physical threat involved. If there was, that was up to his client. The private detective didn't engage in blood work.

He had followed his target for several weeks now, ever since the memorial service for Pete Vine and his wife Dora. They died when their corporate jet crashed in the Mediterranean Sea. All the detective knew was that his target had been a friend of Pete Vine. And he knew that his target was a billionaire.

The detective wasn't given a reason why the target was to be followed, but it really didn't matter. Finding longer paying engagements in this bad economy wasn't easy. Most of the time he had short term assignments working for divorce lawyers, trying to discover evidence of infidelities, financial shenanigans, or anything else that could be used to incriminate a spouse in a court of law. This current engagement was very different and something he didn't fully understand.

His client instructed him to do two things. First was to follow the target and document every movement. For this he had to report to the client at the end of each day, unless there an unusual event.

The second instruction was a bit trickier. He had to plant listening devices anywhere possible to pick up the conversations of the target. But once this was done, someone else was doing the listening. Therefore, he didn't know what they were listening for.

So far he had put microphones in two places; in the target's car and in his office. The one in the office had been the most difficult. The office was in the headquarters of the Unipac Corporation and they had very tight security. But, one evening he slipped in with a group of cleaners and then he completed his task.

The next objective was to put a microphone in the target's home, but he had not yet found an opportunity. There were security cameras around the property and a security company that came and went. His client was starting to complain about the delays and the detective knew that he would have to move soon or he might lose this job.

The detective didn't know who his client was and suspected that the person he talked to on the telephone was an intermediary. The real client was likely to be far up the food chain. That was fine as long as he continued to receive the generous payments into his bank account.

He had been sitting there a long time when he saw his target emerge from the front door of the Unipac headquarters. The detective observed the man as he moved across the parking lot toward a taxi that had pulled up a few minutes before. The man was maybe 5'10" or slightly taller, wore a well fitting dark blue business suit with a red tie, had well trimmed gray hair and he carried himself with a sense of authority. He pulled a wheelie and the detective surmised that the target was going on a trip.

The target got into the taxi, it rolled away, and the detective started up his car and followed.

He wondered why the target had not taken his normal car, which was a standard model company car driven by all Unipac managers. He knew the target was a multi-billionaire and thought it was strange that he wasn't driving a high end luxury brand.

During his research, the detective had learned that the target was known as someone who avoided pretentious things. For sure, his house was very nice and the target stayed at five star hotels, but he had gained a reputation of being wise with his personal finances, as well as with those of his company.

He followed the taxi to the San Jose airport where the target got out and went inside.

The detective rolled past the taxi and pulled into an illegal parking area, engine running, and he called an associate and gave some details.

Airlines don't give out passenger lists, but he knew the associate was able to access airline records.

The detective gave the target's name to his associate.

And then the associate said, "Wait a second."

It was more than a second.

The associate eventually came back on line and said, "He's headed for London and will spend a day there, and then he has a flight to Barcelona." He gave the flight details to the detective.

They hung up and the detective immediately called his client.

The phone rang one time and his client answered and said, "Yes."

The detective said, "He's on his way to Barcelona."

"We know," replied the client. "We already obtained Sam Oliver's flight information. We'll take it from that end."

CHAPTER 2

S am Oliver walked off the airplane and into the Barcelona airport, pulling a wheelie behind him. It had taken him time to adapt to the new contraption given to him by his wife Margaret as a present. He knew that in some ways he was old-school. Some years ago when men started to pull them around he thought they were a bit girlish, but habits change and now they were acceptable. It also meant that for shorter trips he didn't have to check on any luggage, and it was quicker to get through airports.

The Barcelona airport was a modern structure, one that put many large U.S. airports to shame. It had large glass windows that allowed plenty of daylight to come into the airport building, contemporary boutiques for shopping, and easy access from airplanes to the exit.

After going through the passport check and then customs he stepped into the waiting area and scanned across the crowd of people. And then he saw one head sticking above the rest. It was Hank Morgan.

Sam waved and they made eye contact and Hank smiled.

He walked to Hank and they shook hands.

Hank asked. "How was the flight?"

"Not bad," Sam answered. "Good service and on time. And the layover in London did me good. I'm getting too old for long hauls without some kind of a break." Sam knew that a break toward the end of a trip helped with jet lag, one of the things he didn't like about travel. He had experienced a lot of jet lag in his lifetime.

Hank pointed toward the exit and said, "Can I help with anything?"

"Thanks," Sam said, "but I think I can handle the wheelie."

Hank smiled.

They walked side by side toward the exit.

"How was Paris," Sam asked.

"Fabulous," Hank answered. "I saw the painting."

"How was it?" Sam asked.

"I stood there for about an hour, just thinking about it. A reproduction of it was on my wall for six years, but in seeing the original I noticed new things."

Sam knew that Hank went to the Orsay Museum in Paris to see, The Angelus by Jean-François Millet. He also knew about Hank Morgan's background, a kid who grew up in tough neighborhoods in Los Angeles, without parents, bounced around by County Social

Services. He ended up with some very special foster parents who helped him, and then after a stint in the Marines, he went to UCLA and graduated with an MBA. Then he started TechZip, a company that Unipac bought.

There was also an incident with a venture capital company that Sam knew about where Hank had killed three men while in the process of saving two young women and himself.

There was something raw, at times frightening about Hank, but also some tenderness that made him seem vulnerable and likeable. Sam saw qualities in Hank as someone who was good with people and as a potential leader.

And that was part of Sam's motivation for bringing Hank along on this trip. Unipac needed more good leadership as it was in a process of expansion. While Sam had given the reins of Unipac to Paul Kent, his highly capable son-in-law, now they needed to develop more good managers. It was part of succession planning, and Sam knew this was one contribution he could make to the company.

Of course it was uncertain if he could keep Hank in the company. Hank was now a multi-millionaire because of Unipac's purchase of TechZip. But Hank would try to motivate Hank to stay with Unipac, and this trip was a good opportunity. Beyond that, the main objective of the trip was to evaluate if Unipac should buyout the Vine Industries factory in Barcelona.

"Did you see anything else in Paris?" Sam asked.

"I was there three days and saw just about everything," Hank answered. "My legs are worn off."

"Well, now you can rest up while sitting around in conference rooms for a few days." Sam chuckled.

"Are you sure it's going to be rest?" Hank asked.

"For the body yes, but maybe not for the brain." Sam laughed.

They went to the taxi stand where there was an endless row of taxis stretching back as far as the eye could see. There were about ten people in front of them but the line moved quickly.

They got into a taxi and Hank spoke Spanish to the taxi driver instructing him to go to their hotel.

Sam smiled to himself, realizing that Hank had some hidden talents he didn't know about before.

It was late afternoon and the sun was setting over the mountains to the west of Barcelona, giving the mountains and surroundings a pink hue. The taxi sped along and the road joined a freeway heading north toward Barcelona. Rows of old industrial buildings lay on the right and they saw the city in the distance in front of them.

What Sam didn't notice was Hank's glance at a motorcycle following them, being ridden by a man in a black leather jacket with a black helmet and tinted visor.

CHAPTER 3

The following morning Sam had room service bring breakfast to his room

He ate a fresh fruit salad and toast without butter, knowing that Margaret would be proud of him. She was fanatic about healthy food and reproached Sam for his eating habits when he was on business travel. They had an ongoing friendly debate on this, but he knew she was right. He needed to keep his cholesterol in check.

In actual fact he was a trim man and in excellent condition for someone sixty eight years old. He did mild workouts a few times a week and the early morning walks with his dog did him good. And since handing over the leadership of Unipac to Paul Kent it allowed him to step back from the day-to-day pressures.

At the same time it didn't mean there weren't pressures. They just weren't the same as when he was directly leading the company. Now he had time to think more about the long term direction of the company and other strategic things.

Two months ago something happened that dramatically changed the direction of Unipac, resulting from a tragic event.

He remembered it well when one morning he came into the office and Paul Kent joined him and asked if he had heard the news?

"What news," Sam asked.

"I hope this isn't too much of a shock," Paul said, "but Pete and Dora Vine were killed in a plane crash."

It was more than a shock. "How did it happen?" Sam asked in disbelief.

"I don't know all the details, but they were in a corporate jet over the Mediterranean Sea and the jet just disappeared. A search fond nothing but an oil slick and some floating things from the airplane, like a few seats and a doll."

"A doll?" Sam asked.

"Yes. The wife and daughter of one of Pete's best managers were on the airplane. Evidently it was the daughter's doll."

"That's beyond belief... terrible," Sam said, grief beginning to fill his heart.

Pete Vine was one of his best friends. They had both started out at similar times in the Silicon Valley way before the valley was known by that name. They both grew their companies, Unipac and Vine Industries, often partnering together, sometimes competing against each other.

But, it didn't matter if they were competing. They spent a lot of time together, taking fishing trips to the Rocky Mountains and Alaska when they had time, occasionally sailing together, but most often meeting for dinner in the evenings to talk about politics, the economy and technology.

Pete Vine was an excellent manager, one he respected tremendously, who had build up his company from nothing.

Both Unipac and Vine Industries were very strong in the U.S., where both companies had manufacturing plants and sales operations. Outside the U.S. it was different. Unipac had developed most of its international business in Asia, whereas Vine Industries had grown in Europe.

It took Sam several weeks for the deep grief in his heart to subside. Margaret was extremely helpful during that time for she too had lost a friend with Dora Vine.

Then something strange happened. Within a week or two after the death of Pete, the Board of Directors of Vine Industries made a sudden decision to downsize the company by selling off most of its operations. The main reason given was that without the leadership of Pete Vine the vast operations of Vine Industries would fail. The share price had already dropped by fifteen percent upon the news of Pete Vine's death. They said it was a matter of salvaging value for the shareholders.

Sam Oliver thought those reasons were absolutely without a base. This represented the breakup of one of the most successful companies in North America.

The various pieces of Vine Industries were immediately put on the market. Sam met with Paul Kent and the Unipac board of directors and they made a quick decision purchase as many of the Vine Industries businesses as possible. As the majority shareholder in Unipac Sam had a lot to do with this decision. One strong motivating factor was loyalty to his friend. Sam wanted to hold Pete's company together as much as he could.

After making all the financial calculations, Unipac was able to purchase all of the Vine Industries businesses in North America, but other companies came into serious bidding in Europe. The European headquarters of Vine Industries had been based in Paris. Now that office was gone. Sam had heard about a brilliant young manager, Justin Collins, who ran the European operations. He suspected that Pete Vine was grooming him to become the CEO one day. After the sale of the Paris headquarters, Justin Collins had disappeared off the map.

The Europeans were also crying about antitrust saying that Unipac would be too big in Europe, and it would destroy competition. Therefore, most of the European divisions of Vine Industries were bought by EuroVinco a diversified European based company. Then a couple of businesses were bought by a company called GauLux Holding, run by a flamboyant and well know Frenchman by the name of Jacques Gaubert.

Other much smaller companies bought pieces of Vine Industries and in the end it completely vanished.

The only thing left was the factory in Barcelona. No one seemed to want it, although Sam saw value in the products it produced and it complemented Unipac's product lines. He also suspected it might be a good place to put TechZip, the product Unipac had recently purchased from Hank Morgan.

He didn't understand the reasons why European companies didn't take the Barcelona factory. While European politicians had stopped Unipac from coming into Europe in a massive way, they did give the green light for Unipac to acquire the factory. Owning one factory in Europe was anything but anti-competitive, and Sam figured it was act of goodwill to the U.S. government in allowing so called "free" trade.

In the end, Sam detested all the politicking that was taking place and wished governments would just stop trying to run the economy. Hadn't history proved that governments did a miserable job of running economies? Why did they continue to intervene?

So, as Sam sat in his hotel room and finished his morning coffee he wondered what he would discover today at the factory. Was it a good fit for Unipac? And why did the Europeans give the open door for Unipac on this one but not on all the others? Was there someone behind all this pulling the strings?

He looked forward to visit the factory and to see what the day would reveal.

CHAPTER 4

Hank Morgan looked at the scenery as their taxi left Barcelona. They were headed to an area about twenty kilometers northwest of Barcelona where the Vine Industries factory was located.

This trip had been put together so fast that he had no time to prepare for it and he wondered why Sam Oliver had brought him along. It was weird and wonderful to be travelling with this man, a legend in the Silicon Valley and beyond.

In one of his courses at UCLA they had done a case study on Sam Oliver and Unipac, and Hank thought it was amazing to be in a taxi travelling with him. But things had been moving so fast over the previous months, he felt his mind was constantly playing catch up.

Less than a week ago Sam had come to him asking if he would like to go to Barcelona to visit a factory. Hank didn't know what to think. He was loaded with work. His startup company TechZip had been bought by Unipac for a substantial amount of money, and Hank as part of the sale agreement, had to work with Unipac for a year.

At first Hank thought it would be a year of purgatory before he would be free, but he was finding it a challenging and fun experience. It was definitely different than his life in Los Angeles and it was a positive change.

But why had Sam Oliver asked him along?

The reason given was that this factory made products that might be complementary to TechZip and Hank wanted to know if this would be a good place to manufacture his "baby".

Hank knew little more than that. He would have to pick up the pieces as they went along.

They went through a long tunnel and then emerged beyond a small mountain that was to the west of Barcelona.

"May I ask where we are going?" Hank said.

Sam replied, "To a place near the town of Sant Cugat. It's about twenty kilometers from Barcelona."

"It feels like the middle of nowhere," Hank commented.

Sam laughed. "I understand. It's actually an excellent place for manufacturing operations. The main highway from Spain to France goes through that area, so there is great access to the rest of Europe. Many multinational companies have set up in that area."

Indeed, as they drove along, Hank noticed large modern factory buildings with the names of many companies that he recognized. "How do they find qualified people to work here?"

"Spain would surprise you. They have many excellent universities and technical schools in Barcelona, Madrid and other large cities. The workforce is young, educated and dynamic. This area has good transportation access to Barcelona, so many people commute from there."

This was Hank's opportunity to ask questions. He wanted to gain more background as to the purpose of their trip, but he wasn't sure how to ask his next question.

"Ah... may I ask something else?" he said.

"Sure." Sam smiled.

"I was wondering why the Chairman of the Board of Unipac would get involved in this?"

"This?" Sam asked.

"Evaluating a factory. It seems there would be others in Unipac to do this."

Sam smiled and waited a few seconds. "As you know, I'm no longer running the daily operations of the company. Paul Kent handles that. But sometimes he asks me to take on a special assignment, and this one is special."

"How is that?"

"You may not know it, but Pete Vine and I were personal friends for many years. Somehow out of loyalty to my friend I would like to keep his legacy together. He built a great company and it hurts me to see it broken up and sold off in bits and pieces. This trip is personal for me."

Hank felt awkward and sensed it was not the time to ask further questions, although he had many.

The taxi took an off ramp and then pulled in next to a large factory building that had a 'Vine Industries, Sant Cugat' sign on the front.

"It looks like many factory buildings in California," Hank commented.

"It sure does. That was Pete Vine. He pretty much used a standard architecture for his buildings, perfectly designed for efficiency. But an important component was that it had to be employee friendly. He put people first."

When Hank heard this he thought of Sam Oliver. Sam's reputation was that he also put his employees first, always attentive to their needs. In fact, that's what Hank was finding. There was nothing overbearing about the man. He was human and almost simple, yet he knew he was sitting next to one of the world's most brilliant business minds.

They got out of the taxi and Hank felt the warmth of the day. It almost felt like he was in Southern California. There were some eucalyptus trees on one side of the building and the pink oleander bushes and red geraniums were recognizable.

They entered the building and walked to a reception desk.

Sam said to the receptionist, "My name is Sam Oliver and this is Hank Morgan. We are here to see Mr. Mateu."

She smiled and Hank noticed she was young and pretty, and there was something energetic about her.

"Yes, yes," she said. "He is expecting you."

She made a call and in two minutes a man walked into the reception area. He was about 5'8' and wore gray slacks and a blue shirt with a blue stripped tie. He didn't wear a suit jacket.

He smiled and shook Sam's hand.

"It is nice to meet you Mr. Oliver," the man said. My name is Ramon Mateu."

Sam said, "Likewise, it is a pleasure to meet you. May I introduce you to Hank Morgan who will be assisting me during my visit?"

Ramon Mateu turned to Hank and shook his hand, looking up at him.

Hank suspected that at six foot four inches and two hundred and forty pounds, he was an interesting sight to many people.

Ramon Mateu said, "Could you follow me. We will start in a conference room."

They followed Mateu and entered what looked to be the administrative wing of the factory, a long corridor of offices with glass walls so that you could see into the offices. Hank noticed maybe thirty or forty people working behind desks.

Ramon Mateu stopped and said, "These are our administrative offices." He paused. "There's just one thing." His eyes looked down and he hesitated. "There was a change of plans. Things are moving so fast these days and with so much uncertainty about what is going to happen to us, it seems there are other companies interested in this operation here."

"What do you mean?" Sam asked.

"It was decided that this is to be a general information day where we present the factory to all bidders. Then individual questions can be answered in the days to come."

"Who decided that?" Sam asked.

Hank noticed that Sam's eyes narrowed. He suddenly saw toughness in the man.

"I don't know?" Mateu answered. "An administrative assistant working for the Board of Directors of Vine Industries called me and said that we were to present the company to all bidders. So, I just followed instructions."

"So the other companies are here?" Sam asked.

"Yes," Mateu answered.

"How many are there?"

"Two others."

"This is highly unusual," Sam stated.

"I don't know," Mateu replied. "I'm just doing what I was told."

"I understand," Sam said. "So let's go meet the competition."

Hank followed Sam and Ramon Mateu down the corridor realizing that something unexpected had happened, although he wasn't sure what it was. He didn't know how these buyouts worked, but from the look on Sam's face, it seemed unusual to be meeting in the same room as other interested parties.

Now, more than ever he wondered what he was doing here. He had absolutely no experience in any of this and he was not certain what would happen next.

This was way beyond anything he was familiar with in growing up in Los Angeles.

CHAPTER 5

From the expression on Sam's face, Hank was cautious when they entered the conference room. He wasn't sure what he was supposed to do or say, so he decided to keep a low profile until Sam would let him know what was going on.

It was a good sized conference room. Besides himself, Sam and Ramon Mateu, Hank counted eight men and one woman in the room. He guessed the woman to be between forty to forty five years old.

On one side of the room there was a table covered with a white table cloth. It had a small bouquet of flowers, large thermos bottles with coffee and tea, as well as croissants and bottles of juice.

In the middle of the room there was a large long conference table. He saw that most of the places had been taken because there were personal papers small laptops, and electronic Tablets positioned by most of the chairs. Two empty places remained at the end of the table, farthest away from the presentation area.

That was okay for Hank, as it would allow him to watch the others around the table. But he still didn't know what Sam was thinking.

Introductions were made. The woman's name was Francina Bissom and she was the Human Resources Manager of the factory. Five of the men held different management and supervisory positions mostly having to do with various aspects of production, but one man was responsible for sales and marketing.

One man was from GauLux Holding and his name was Pierre Dubois. He was a small round Frenchman who wore wire-rim glasses, a suit that seemed one size too small, and a purple and red tie. He squinted through dark beady eyes and had an expressionless face.

The other two were from a company called Dicio Partners with a headquarters in Frankfurt, but with offices in many major cities in Europe. Their names were Hugo Aaron, a small dark Spanard, and Otto Walther, a large German who appeared to love his beer.

Hank had never heard of GauLux Holding or Dicio Partners.

Hank saw that Sam was very polite when introductions were made and he followed Sam's example. Pierre Dubois from GauLux Holding was based in Nice, France. Otto Walther, was from the Dicio offices in Frankfurt and Hugo Aaron was from Dicio in Madrid. Hank thought he should speak Spanish with the Hugo Aaron, but for some reason he held back from doing so.

It seemed that everyone in the room treated Sam Oliver with a high degree of respect. He overheard two of factory managers talking between themselves in Spanish, almost in wonder that the famous Sam Oliver would be joining this meeting.

They took their places around the conference table and Sam Oliver took his jacket off and hung it on the back of his chair. Hank did the same. The men from GauLux and Dicio kept their jackets on.

The meeting began with an introduction from Ramon Mateu and then there were long detailed presentations going through the financial figures, sales plans, markets, products, technology and production. Each presentation was interrupted with numerous questions that went into great detail.

Francina Bissom, the Human Resources Manager, gave an update on the people in the factory, their general backgrounds, education, language groups, recruitment, and some particular things about hiring practices in Spain. It turned out that there were slightly over eight hundred people working in the factory and in outlying operations.

Sam Oliver asked few questions, but when he did they seemed to be more profound than all the others.

The presentations consisted of one detailed slide after another and Hank was relieved when lunch was served in the room, buffet style on the long table with the white table cloth.

After lunch Hank felt drowsy and he thought jet lag was getting to him. He had never been in a different time zone from California. In fact, he had never been out of that state, except for a few trips to Tijuana, Mexico. Now he was nine time zones away and he could feel the effects of jet lag for the first time in his life. While he had been in Europe for several days, the tiredness was still hitting him.

It was difficult for him to just sit there without any movement, but he was resolved that he would listen as carefully as possible to see what he could learn.

During the afternoon coffee break he went to the rest room. In returning to the conference room he walked down a hallway and he heard someone speaking Spanish just around the corner. He heard Unipac mentioned so stopped to listen.

One person said, "You better present this in our favor."

"I can't," the other voice said.

Hank recognized it to be the voice of Ramon Mateu. The other was the voice of Hugo Aaron, the Dicio Partners representative from Madrid.

"You know what will happen," Aaron said.

"Please. Can't you find another way," Mateu implored.

"You do what we say," said Aaron.

Hank went around the corner and saw Ramon Mateu nodding to the Dicio Partners man.

They stopped talking until Hank passed by.

* * *

At the end of the afternoon Ramon Mateu stood in front and began to summarize the day and was about to close when Hugo Aaron raised his hand.

Mateu said, "Yes."

Aaron said, "Are there any serious issues that we should be aware of?"

Mateu said, "Ah… maybe one or two."

"Such as," Aaron said.

"Well, it was touched upon by Francina our human resources manager, but there is industrial relations unrest. Since the breakup of Vine Industries there is a fear that jobs may be lost. Therefore the motivation of the staff has been impacted and production has slowed. And it has given an opportunity for union leaders to gain power. We don't know where this will end."

"What is the other problem," Aaron asked.

"There are rumors that the European Union may block the sale if it is not to their liking. Therefore it could become expensive for a potential buyer if they have to hire lawyers to fight this in Brussels and Strasbourg."

Hank noticed that Otto Walther, the German from Dicio glanced quickly at Sam Oliver and then back at the Aaron.

Hugo Aaron nodded.

★ ★ ★

The meeting ended for the day. It was announced that Ramon Mateu would lead a tour of the factory the following morning. From then on there would be individual meetings scheduled with the interested companies to answer any questions.

Sam and Hank went to the reception area where they hired a taxi.

They went outside and waited.

Hank asked, "How do you think it went?"

"Very unsettling," Sam said.

"Why is that?" Hank asked.

Having GauLux and Dicio there was definitely unexpected.

"Do you know of these companies?" Hank asked.

"Yes, I do," Sam answered.

"What do you know?"

"GauLux Holding makes a lot of consumer household products like vacuums and mixers, and they make some luxury products like perfumes and clothing. It is a very strong company in the European markets. The company is run by Jacques Gaubert, a Frenchman that seems to have his fingers into everything from sports teams to politics."

"And Dicio?"

"Well both companies are known to be cutthroat in working with others but Dicio is way out there."

"What do you mean?" Hank asked.
"Bad news... very bad news. These guys are ruthless."

CHAPTER 6

The fact that GauLux and Dicio were there unsettled Sam. There had been no warning and he didn't like it. Of the two companies, Dicio worried him the most. They had a reputation that caused the business world to flinch. This meant that their time in Barcelona would be more complex than he originally expected. Unipac was now up against aggressive competition and he would need to be very careful as they moved forward.

The taxi came, Sam gave the name of their hotel, and the taxi started to move.

"What do you mean by bad news," Hank asked.

Sam held a finger to his lips and then pointed at the driver in such a way that the driver couldn't see him.

Hank nodded.

Sam saw that Hank understood it was better to speak in confidentiality for there was no way to know if the driver spoke English or who he would be reporting to. Better to be safe than sorry.

The events of the day troubled Sam, not only that there were other companies in the bidding, but more so who they were.

He wondered why they would want this factory?

GauLux Holding was primarily involved in consumer products used in homes. The Vine Industries Sant Cugat factory specialized in components and products that were mostly used in computing, telecommunications and industrial applications. There just didn't seem to be a fit with GauLux and the factory.

For this, the small Frenchman Pierre Dubois seemed to be out of place. He rarely said anything during the meeting.

Dicio was something different, a group of partners that were known as slash and burn artists, buying any asset they could for a low value, and then stripping it and selling the pieces. They had no regard for people and if Dicio made a profit while thousands of people lost their jobs, it didn't matter.

Dicio was a company with a vicious reputation, almost frightening. The rumor was that they did anything to achieve their objectives. They used intimidation, law suits and anything else to achieve their end. One story Sam had heard was that a European journalist investigating Dicio just disappeared. Some law agencies began to look into it, but it turned out that influential politicians were protecting the company. Therefore the news media backed off and Dicio had a free hand in Europe.

Of the two companies, the eight hundred workers at the Vine Industries factory should worry most about Dicio.

One of the things that bothered Sam was that the Board of Directors at Vine Industries had given him the go ahead to pursue the Barcelona factory purchase. For the purchase of all the U.S. components of Vine Industries things had gone relatively well and there were no major problems.

Now, why had the board allowed these two other companies to get into the bidding for the factory?

The European Union had also given clearance for Unipac to pursue this purchase. Now these European companies were unexpectedly competing for the factory. Was there someone pulling the strings of the European politicians?

Sam questioned why GauLux and Dicio would get involved? Was there some special product or technology they wanted, one that Sam didn't know about, or was there something else?

Sam reflected back on the day's presentations looking for clues. Hank had been quiet for much of the day, but maybe he spotted something. They planned to go out to dinner together in Barcelona. Hopefully they would have an opportunity to talk confidentially.

All Sam knew was that they would be in Barcelona longer than he first expected.

CHAPTER 7

Hoerst Krause, the Managing Director of Dicio, put down the telephone, swiveled around in his chair and gazed down at the lights of Frankfurt below. He was satisfied with the call and felt they were making progress.

The Dicio Partners headquarters were in the top floor of one of the tallest office buildings in Frankfurt which gave him a magnificent view. He reflected on what had been shared. Now they must carefully manage events over the next few days to achieve a successful outcome.

Otto Walther, one of his managers attending the meeting in Barcelona, had given him an update. As expected, Sam Oliver had shown up and the day had consisted of a series of presentations informing the attendees about the operations.

Otto Walther and Hugo Aaron had also been successful in persuading the director of the factory to highlight some of the issues being faced by the factory, even though the issues were a bit exaggerated.

The objective was to raise doubts in Sam Oliver's mind. Now he needed to call his outside business partner to review how things should go from here.

He dialed a local Frankfurt number and a man answered.

Krause said, "Karl, this is Hoerst. Things are progressing in Barcelona."

He was speaking with Karl Schubach, one of the highest ranking people in EuroVinco. EuroVinco was a European conglomerate with diversified headquarter offices in Frankfurt, London and Nice, France. They spoke German with each other and Krause gave an update.

"*Wunderbar*, now we take the next steps."

"Yes. Although, we should keep a small degree of flexibility." Flexibility was not something usually attributed to German business leaders. They were more inclined to form a plan and then stick with it.

"Why is that?" Schubach asked.

"We should wait to see the direction that Unipac will take."

"We know the outcome we desire," Schubach said.

"I know, but we can get there through a number of means." Krause stated. His plan was to first plant doubts about the factory, so that Unipac would wonder if this was a viable investment for the company. If they progressed, then they would use other means."

"As long as we meet the objectives," Schubach stated.

This was understood between them. The goal was for Dicio to purchase the factory, but the Frankfurt division of EuroVinco would be a silent partner. They would sell off some of the assets of the factory, and EuroVinco would end up owning what was left. Through this, both Dicio and EuroVinco Frankfurt would make a significant profit.

Their business arrangement had come together very fast. Even though the two men had known each other for years and had worked together on a couple of other business deals, this one was put together with lightning speed.

They had monitored the developments after the fall of Vine Industries where Unipac had purchased all of the U.S. assets of the company. EuroVinco had ended up with some of the European assets, but not all of them. EuroVinco was smaller than Unipac and it didn't have the same strong financial platform.

They understood that Unipac needed the Sant Cugat factory. First, was because Unipac did not have a particularly strong presence in Europe. The Barcelona factory would help strengthen Unipac's position in this regard.

The second reason was emotional. Sam Oliver had been a close friend of Pete Vine and there was a desire of Sam Oliver to hold Vine Industries together because of that friendship.

Schubach and Krause had analyzed this and knew that both reasons could be used to their advantage. If EuroVinco ended up owning this factory, then they could dangle it in front of Sam Oliver in a plan for EuroVinco to gain an even bigger prize.

The European Union had given the go ahead for Unipac to purchase the factory, but in the mean time Dicio had discovered that there were some hidden assets in the factory and it was at that point that they decided on their new plan.

Schubach said, "So the next step is to destabilize Sam Oliver."

"That's correct," Krause answered. "We will continue to plant doubts in his mind… and we will make sure he has a miserable experience in Barcelona."

Schubach gave a small almost indistinguishable laugh. "That's great. I wish I could be there to see it."

"We have people on the ground. Oh yes, there is just one thing."

"What's that?" Schubach asked.

"Sam Oliver is travelling with one of his managers to help with the evaluation. His name is Hank Morgan."

"Do you know anything about him?"

"Not much, other than the fact that he recently joined Unipac. Unipac bought his company."

"Let's find out who he is," Schubach stated.

"I'll work on it," Krause replied.

"But make sure this Hank Morgan gets the same welcome treatment as Sam Oliver. If he's part of the decision process, then they need to come to the same negative conclusion."

"Definitely," Krause stated.

"Okay. Keep me updated," Schubach said.

They hung up.

Hoerst Krause knew that Schubach was similar to him in one respect. They would both do anything to achieve their goal, and that meant anything. It was reassuring to know he had a business partner that would use any means to justify the end.

CHAPTER 8

They got back to the hotel and Sam motioned for them to go into the coffee shop and they found an empty table in a corner.

They sat down and Sam said, "I'm sorry about the silence in the car, but you never know if the taxi driver understands English or who he is working for. Over the years I've learned to beware before you share."

"I understand," Hank said. "You mentioned that Dicio was bad news. What do you mean?"

"That company has a terrible reputation. They are asset strippers of the worst kind. They are known to go after any company where they can make a profit. First they will do anything to drive the price of the company down. Then they scare away any competitors. After buying a company they strip out the assets and sell them to the highest bidders. It's a method that produces exorbitant returns for them. I have no problem with making a profit if it's done in the right way. The problem is that they don't care who they hurt in the process.

"Why would they want this factory in Sant Cugat?" Hank asked.

"To be honest, I don't know." Sam replied.

Hank was still, then asked, "Dicio is a strange name for a company. What does it mean?"

"It's Latin. It means dominion or perhaps, power, a very fitting name for what they attempt to do."

"I guess they chose the right name," Hank said. "And what about GauLux? Why are they here? Dubois, that Frenchman just sits there and doesn't say anything. It just seems he is there as a spectator."

"I have the same impression. This is another mystery," Sam said. "Hopefully we will gain some answers over the next few days."

Hank hesitated for a moment looking down at the table. "I have a question."

Sam looked at him. "Sure. Go ahead."

"Why am I here? I don't think I added much value to the meeting today."

"Like I said, my experience tells me that the Sant Cugat factory might be a good fit for TechZip. They make bar code readers and devices used in telecommunications. That's the kind of expertise one needs in making virtual inventory monitoring devices. Think of TechZip."

"Still, I think you have broader considerations than that," Hank said, "and I'm not sure how I can help."

"I'd suggest you use this as a learning experience," Sam said. "Sometimes you learn the most when you step out of your comfort zone."

Hank laughed. "This certainly is. It's the first time I've ever been out of California, and it's a totally different world than the streets of L.A."

"One thing," Sam said. "In knowing Dicio they will throw a lot at us over the coming days. Be ready."

"Ready for what?" Hank asked.

"Be ready for anything. As I said, they are ruthless and I mean that in every sense of the word."

CHAPTER 9

At seven thirty Hank went down to the hotel lobby and joined Sam. He was looking forward to see Barcelona after being cooped up in a conference room all day.

They took a taxi to the Placa Catalunya, a large open area in the middle of Barcelona. Many consider it to be the city center. It has fountains and statues, and it was a starting point for major avenues that fanned out across Barcelona. It was a gathering place for political events and for celebrating the victories of their sports teams.

They got out of the taxi and Hank looked around at the immense square. There was nothing like it that he knew of in Los Angeles. At the same time things didn't feel totally strange. He saw posters, most in the Catalan language, but some in Spanish. Somehow, being surrounded by these Latin languages made him feel at home. Until his early teens he had grown up in Hispanic areas of Los Angeles and it was there that he had mastered the Spanish language.

He reflected on what Sam had said about Dicio and then he reflected on the conversation earlier in the day between Ramon Mateu and Hugo Aaron from Dicio. He remembered Mateu's hesitation, even a look of fear in his eyes. And, Aaron was asking Mateu to do something, to present something in Dicio's favor. Hank wondered what that was.

His thoughts were interrupted when he saw Ramon Mateu walking toward them. Next to Ramon was Francina Bissom, the Human Resources Manger who had been at the meeting during the day. Next to her was a younger woman.

Mateu waved and walked up to them and everyone shook hands and Ramon introduced the younger woman.

"This is Carme Cesca-Anglesa," he said. She works with Francina and is responsible for recruitment. I thought she could give some information on the profile of people we are hiring."

Carme shook hands with everyone and Hank glanced at her and saw that she was very attractive. Her hair was blond and she had blue eyes, which he thought unusual for someone from Spain. Most of the Hispanics he had grown up with had dark hair and dark eyes. And, Carme was taller than average.

She wore black slacks, a blue cotton blouse, a light jacket with embellished sequins on one shoulder, and a purple and pastel silk scarf. She had a nice figure and a smile that made Hank relax.

Mateu said, "Our restaurant is in that direction, down Las Ramblas," as he pointed to one street that went off from the Placa Catalunya.

They crossed a street and began walking down a wide pedestrian street. It was crowded with families and couples. Mateu explained that this was a very popular street for people to take a stroll in the evenings and on the weekends. He said many tourists came here when they visited Barcelona.

Mateu pointed down the street and said, "At the end down there by the sea there is a large statue honoring Cristabol Colon for when he left on one of his trips to the New World. I think you call him Christopher Columbus."

Hank noticed many shops on the street, small boutiques selling everything from newspapers, to jewelry to clothing.

They walked five minutes and turned down a side street where Mateu led them into a restaurant.

Hank almost hit is head on the door going in and Mateu laughed and said, "This restaurant has been here for over three hundred years. People were not as tall as you when they build the place."

Hank noticed a twinkle in Carme's eye.

Inside the restaurant was a large room with tables. Openings led off to smaller rooms on one side. The restaurant was almost empty.

"Don't worry," Mateu said. "By ten o'clock this place will be full. People in Spain tend to eat dinner later in the evening than you do in America. When I made the reservation they said they would be able to serve earlier. They are used to having visitors from other countries."

The waiter led them into a side room with fewer tables. The ceiling was vaulted and they were seated at a large round oak table that seemed to be as old as the restaurant itself.

Hank followed Ramon Mateu's lead and ordered a starter salad with strips of filet of duck, and then a main course of roasted lamb. They had red wine called Crianza that came from an area somewhat south of Barcelona, and for desert had Crema Catalana. It came in a round pottery dish and was rich and creamy with a crunchy sugar crust on top. Mateu explained that it was the Catalan version of the French crème brulée. The food was a delight for Hank, as he reflected back on his typical spaghetti meals at his one bedroom apartment in Venice Beach.

The conversation roamed to many topics including the history of Catalonia to the famous Football Club of Barcelona. Indeed Hank knew it as 'football' rather than soccer, because of his growing up with Spanish speaking kids in L.A.

Hank saw that Sam was totally at ease with everyone and with their surroundings. At one point Sam said, "May I ask a business question?"

"For sure Mr. Oliver," Mateu responded.

Sam smiled. "Please call me Sam." Then he asked. "Today when Francina was making her presentation she said that you were looking for engineers, not only those specializing in computer electronics, but also in radio frequencies and optics. That's quite a combination of technical knowledge. Where do you find those experts?"

"At the UPC," Francina answered.

"What's that?" Sam asked.

"The Universitat Politècnica de Catalunya. Some English speaking people call it Barcelona Tech. It is a leading technical university with a very high reputation around the world."

"Yes, I've heard of it," Sam said.

"That's where we get many people that work at the factory," Francina said. "In fact, the Vine Industries factory has a large research building that is next to the university."

When she said that Hank noticed that Mateu's eyes widen and a frown formed on his forehead.

"I wasn't aware of that," Sam said.

"Oh, it is nothing," Mateu said. "Just a place where we train up some engineers with our technologies."

Francina started to say something, but Mateu gave her a quick glance and she refrained herself. Likewise, Carme didn't say anything.

Hank couldn't remember the research facility being mentioned during any of the presentations.

The meal ended and Sam paid the bill. They left the restaurant, went back to Las Ramblas, and headed back toward the Placa Catalunya where Sam and Hank would get a taxi back to the hotel.

On the way there an older man with a gray beard man approached them with a map. He walked up to Sam holding the map out and moved it right up to Sam's chest.

"Do you know where I can find the cathedral," He asked, speaking English with a Spanish accent.

Sam automatically looked down at the map.

Two other men who seemed to be with the man walked close to Sam and leaned over to look at the map. One had a black mustache and three day beard. The other wore a tight fitting blue T-shirt. His hear was close cut and he was muscular.

Hank immediately knew what was going on. He had seen this trick used a thousand times in Los Angeles.

He saw the hand of one of the man with the mustache reach into Sam's back pocket where he removed Sam's walled.

With lightning speed Hank reached over and grabbed the man's hand and he twisted the hand and the wallet fell to the ground and then Hank twisted some more. He felt a snap in the man's wrist and the man screamed out.

The muscular man on the other side of Sam yelled something and moved around toward Hank and then took a swing at him. Hank stepped back, avoiding the swing and then he unloaded a hard left uppercut to the man's jaw. There was a loud crack and the man fell to the ground.

The first man that had the map saw what was happening and he sprinted off, followed by the man with the injured wrist.

Hank reached down to the ground, took the wallet and handed it to Sam.

Francina and Carme looked at Hank in horror.

Hanks eyes followed the men as they disappeared around a corner and he wondered if he should go after them.

CHAPTER 10

The following morning they met in the hotel lobby Sam said, "That was an unusual evening last night. How do you feel?"

"Feel?" Hank asked.

"About those pick pockets."

"It happened. The guy took a swing, so what could I do?"

"Well, first let me thank you," Sam said. "But, there's something more."

"What's that?"

"This morning I spoke with the police officer, Captain Valls."

Several police officers had arrived after the pick pocketing incident. They had called an ambulance to take the muscular thief to the hospital and then they questioned everyone to understand what had happened.

There were no charges against Hank for hitting the thief as it was a clear case of self defense. The pick pocket was also known by the police, so there was no pity for him. The lead policeman, a Captain Valls, had given his card to Sam.

"What did Captain Valls say," Hank asked.

"He went to the hospital to interview the guy with the broken jaw. The thief was given drugs for the pain and that put him in a talkative mood. It seems someone hired them to steal my wallet."

"What? That's strange. Who and why would someone do that?" Hank asked.

"Good question," Sam said. "And let me say it again. Thanks for what you did."

$\star\ \star\ \star$

When they got to the factory they waited in the reception area where a production manager would meet them to give a tour of the factory.

Sam looked forward to see the factory. He had seen thousands of factories in his lifetime, yet each one was unique. He was always impressed at the multitude of different ways that raw materials could be formed into products that gave benefits to people.

Unipac had many factories in the U.S., Asia and Mexico. Sam was thankful that his company could provide employment for people where they could then feed their families and send their children to school. He knew that factory work was not always the most rewarding, where many jobs were repetitive. Therefore he did everything he could to bring variety into the routines through the regular rotation of people. He also gave the quality control responsibilities to the workers, so they had a say in how to improve processes. In Unipac's factories the workers were given breaks in comfortable areas and that all facilities were modern and clean, from the cafeteria to the rest rooms. Sam knew that Pete Vine had followed a similar way of managing people.

As they waited, Sam carefully reflected on the events of the previous evening, especially the pick pocketing incident. What was particularly troubling was what he heard this morning from the policeman, Captain Valls. Hank had asked the right question. Who and why would someone do that?

Sam didn't have an answer and that bothered him. Therefore he reflected on the bigger picture to see if he could find any clues.

The Unipac purchase of the Sant Cugat factory was part of a much bigger business play. Through Sam's leadership, Unipac had purchased all the Vine Industry pieces in North America, but the European Union had stopped Unipac from buying the businesses in Europe.

That bothered Sam. He knew that a lot of the Vine Industries business units were integrated between North America and Europe. They shared in product development and leveraged across geographical sales channels. If you broke them apart they would be less effective.

Unipac had paid above market value for the North American business units, yet Sam felt it was the right thing to do. And it was also a good strategic business decision in that it allowed Unipac to expand its range of products and services. But, Unipac wouldn't get the full benefits without owning the corresponding European pieces.

In the broad scope of everything, the Sant Cugat factory was a very small piece. Why would anyone be bothered to if Unipac owned the factory?

Sam just couldn't figure out the motivation of someone to hire pick pockets to steal his wallet. There was nothing special in that wallet that anyone else wouldn't carry; some money, a couple of credit cards, a photo of Margaret his wife, and that was about it.

What surprised him was the way Hank had handled the pick pockets. In a very quick movement Hank had grabbed the pick pocket's hand, twisted it in an expert way, and it seemed that Hank may have broken the fellow's wrist.

Then the second thief had taken a swing at Hank and in a split second the thief was knocked out cold. Hank had reacted so swiftly.

It seemed he didn't even think about it. Then afterwards the calmness in Hank was almost unsettling, as though this was an everyday event.

Sam knew about Hank's background, an orphan, growing up in tough areas of Los Angeles, two years in the Marines, his work as a lifeguard for Los Angeles Country, and then his work with Robert Campbell in developing TechZip.

He was also aware that Hank had a aggressive side. A venture capital company had illegally tried to take over TechZip, they had kidnapped Hank and two women and threatened to kill them. Hank had defended them and three men ended up dead.

In all of Sam's dealings with Hank over the past months they had never talked about it. How did Hank feel about this? It was hard to tell.

Above everything, Sam was thankful that Hank was there last night. On his own he would not have been able to do anything against the three thieves, even if he would have noticed that his wallet was being taken. They were so slick about it.

Sam could hardly recollect the event because it all happened so quickly and Hank had it all under control. Sam was gaining a greater appreciation for the young man and he was glad that Hank was along on this trip.

He thought about the people who hired the thieves and it all just didn't make sense. He decided the only thing he could do was to stay cautious.

As he thought about the evening he remembered what Francina had said about a research facility over by the technical university. Ramon Mateu had acted strange when she mentioned it, even down playing it as a training facility.

Sam decided that they should take a look at the facility.

As they waited, a number of people arrived, although Sam realized that the factory workers would be entering through another entrance.

The production manager arrived, they shook hands and he led them in an opposite direction from the administrative wing where they had spent the previous day.

The people from GauLux and Dicio did not join them, so the tour was given to Sam and Hank alone. They were told that Dicio was meeting with Ramon Mateu. Pierre Dubois from GauLux was somewhere in the building, but no one was sure where.

The factory was an immense building with a seamless integration of conveyor belts that moved electronic pieces from one point to another.

Robots were spinning things, cutting them, screwing things together, soldering them and doing a multitude of other actions. People filled the gaps, playing essential roles in assembling, inspecting, and monitoring machines.

As Sam and Hank moved through the building, people looked at them but mainly at Sam whose reputation undoubtedly had gone before him. It was like a country president or film star was in their midst. Then they would stare at Hank, this taller, broader assistant who looked more like he belonged on a rugby club than an electronics company.

★ ★ ★

At lunch time they went to the cafeteria where they had arranged to meet Francina and Carme. They waited at the entrance where Hank saw factory workers entering, taking trays, selecting their food and then going to the checkout. Things flowed efficiently, just like what he saw in the factory.

Hank wondered how TechZip would fit into this and even though he had sold his company to Unipac he still felt responsibility for the product. It was still his baby.

One condition in the buy out contract stipulated that Hank was required to work for Unipac for one year, to help with the transition. That was often a standard part of the contract when one company purchased another, especially a startup company. Often the new technology existed mainly inside someone's head, so the purchasing company wanted to make sure that the new technology was well integrated so they didn't lose their investment.

Unipac had paid a significant price for TechZip, which was almost unbelievable for Hank. From one moment to the next he had gone from poverty to unbelievable riches. The buyout price was five hundred million dollars and twenty percent of that had gone to his business partner Robert Campbell, the technical brains behind TechZip. Hank had received the rest.

Robert was well experienced in these kinds of things and he introduced Hank to trusted accountants and tax experts who knew how to conserve the wealth. Other experienced investment advisors took over the management of the wealth, investing it into stocks, bonds and other investment instruments.

Half of the buyout was in cash and the other half was in shares of

Unipac. That meant that Hank was now had a significant holding in Unipac, although no where close to the billions owned by Sam. At the same time, it meant that Hank wanted the very best for the company, as well as for his baby, TechZip.

The main functionality of TechZip was virtual inventory taking. That probably didn't sound too exciting to end consumers, but it was revolutionary for companies. Fundamentally it meant that people didn't have to waste time going around physically counting their inventory. A small patch would be stuck to each product and a sensor would pick up a signal and track the product. It was like a bar code reader that scanned the code remotely.

The applications for this were endless. For instance, in a grocery store employees wouldn't have to go from shelf to shelf counting cereal boxes and other items. By just walking down the aisles the reader would pick up the electronic signals.

This represented a huge saving in time and a giant leap forward in accuracy.

The question was how the Sant Cugat factory converged with TechZip? Sam Oliver had said that this factory might be a good place to produce TechZip. Hank was beginning to see the possibility.

The factory made a number of different products and the people here seemed to have some unique competencies. One of them was in wireless technology. They made antennas used in everything from radios to wireless routers. That was a the key component of TechZip.

The 'patch' developed by Robert Campbell sent out an electronic signal. It wasn't very strong, but enough to be picked up not far away through a wireless device. If the signal from the patch or the sensitivity of the wireless reader could be strengthened, then it would enhance the capabilities of TechZip.

Maybe that's what Sam was thinking?

Hank knew he could not be of much assistance in making the financial calculations to buy the Barcelona factory, but he could be of help in evaluating the fit for TechZip. Maybe the factory had some useful technology here that was useful. Robert Campbell from Campbell Labs in Los Angeles had been the technology brains in developing TechZip and now he wished that Robert was here to make the evaluation.

Down the hall he saw Francina and Carme approaching them. Carme walked with a long stride, a tall slender woman with curves in all the right places.

Hank thought he saw a sense of hesitation when Carme looked at him. He was sure that his actions with the thieves the previous night may have frightened her.

But what else could he have done? Perhaps he could have been a little less brutal. He may have broken one guy's wrist and he definitely broke the other guy's jaw. He felt stupid, knowing that he had again pushed things too far. That was his problem, to employ a sledge hammer when a tack hammer would be sufficient.

He understood why women would shy away from him. Isn't that what happened with Sharlee, and just about every other girl he had gotten close to?

They took trays, selected their food and then Francina took them through the checkout. Rather than eating in one of the smaller dining rooms reserved for guests, Sam had suggested that they eat in the main dining area.

Hank knew that Sam liked to be close to people.

The main dining area was a noisy place and Hank heard people speaking different languages, Catalan, Spanish, French and some English.

Conversations seem to quiet as they walked by. The word was probably out that the famous Sam Oliver was in the building and that Unipac was thinking to purchase the factory. Change makes people nervous and Hank suspected that these people were wondering what would happen with their jobs.

They took places at the end of a long table.

Sam asked, "Is Ramon meeting with Dicio?"

Francina looked hesitant. "Yes, with Otto Walther and Hugo Aaron They are discussing details."

Sam smiled. "What are our chances?"

Francina answered. "It is very complicated. Two weeks ago it was certain that our factory would join Unipac. Everyone was extremely happy when we heard that because we knew Unipac's reputation. Now we are less certain about who will own the factory."

"Why did Dicio jump into the game?" Sam asked.

"We don't know," Francina answered.

Carme interrupted. "We also don't know why GauLux Holding showed up. They don't make anything that uses our components. We would prefer Unipac."

Hank saw her eyes widen, expressing concern.

"We will do our best," Sam stated.

They ate their lunch and it was Hank's chance to ask some questions about the factory and their products.

The factory had a marketing group that was responsible for selling their products. They made components and did have some finished products which were mainly sold under the brands of electronic retailers. Most of their sales were in Europe, but they also sold in North America and Asia.

Their main competition was from companies in Asia where production costs were less. At the same time, their key competitive advantage was in technology and with they stayed one step ahead of the competition.

Carme mentioned that the R&D lab by the technical university was instrumental in developing new products.

Sam said, "Last night Ramon said that facility was mainly used for training new people. Are they also doing research and development?"

Francina jumped in. "A little. But that's where we integrate some of the graduates from the university."

Hank sensed she was deflecting Sam's question. He remembered how Mateu had glanced at here last night. Hank spoke Spanish, but more so he understood Latin glances and body language which was a large part of communication. He caught things that most Anglo-Saxons would not. The message from Mateu was to be careful what you say.

Carme seemed to question Francina's statement. "Well no. There is some interesting research going on over there."

Francina's eyes narrowed at Carme, just enough to communicate to her to not contradict her boss.

Hank caught this. From it he suspected that something was being discussed between Ramon Mateu and Francina, that Carme didn't know about.

They went on to other topics and when the meal was finished Sam said, "I think we'd like to do a little bit of management by wandering around. We'd like to be set free to talk with people."

Francina nodded. "Ramon said that you should be free to talk with anyone."

* * *

For the next couple of hours Sam and Hank wandered around the factory spending time at the coffee machine talking with people. Sam took the lead, as he was an old hand at this kind of thing.

He said that if you want to understand the pulse of a company, you went to the coffee area. It was there that information was shared from one person to another, where rumors spread and secrets divulged.

After an hour in the coffee area Sam nodded to Hank and they walked away.

"What do you think?" Sam asked.

"People seem to be scared," Hank replied.

"You got it right. It's normal whenever there is a change, but in this case it seems more magnified than usual."

"Where do we go from here?" Hank asked.

"I think we should visit the R&D building over near the university."

"Did you notice the same thing as me?" Hank asked.

"Such as?"

"Ramon is trying to hold something back and he has instructed Francina to not share some things."

"You are perceptive," Sam said. "I like that."

"Where is it and how do we get there?"

"I think there is someone we should ask to take us there," Sam stated.

"Who is that?"

"Carme. I don't think she knows what is being discussed between Ramon and Francina."

Hank realized that Sam was seeing the same things he was, perhaps even more. The experienced billionaire was indeed an old fox.

CHAPTER 11

Hoerst Krause at the Dicio headquarters in Frankfurt called Otto Walther in Barcelona. He was anxious to find out how things were progressing. A successful outcome at the Sant Cugat factory represented a profitable return for Dicio.

"Where are they?" Krause asked.

"They are in a car going into Barcelona?" Walther answered.

"Do you know where they are going?"

"No, but Paco, the man on the motorcycle is following them? They are with one of the women from Human Resources, someone who reports directly to Francina Bissom, the Human Resources Manager."

"Why are they with her?"

"Again, I don't know. She joined them for dinner last night. Maybe it's something to do with that." Walther hesitated then said, "Something unexpected happened last night."

"What do you mean?" Krause asked.

Otto Walther gave an update on what occurred with the pick pockets, two being injured with broken bones.

"It is unfortunate, but it doesn't matter," commented Krause. "The objective is to unsettle Sam Oliver to such an extent that Unipac backs out of the purchase. The pick pocketing incident is only a beginning."

Hoerst Krause was a calculating man. Every time tactics did not work out as planned, he adapted the strategy, like a chess player that loses a pawn. The important thing was checkmate and he knew that he was a very good chess player.

In this case they would increase the pressure to such an extent that Sam Oliver would walk away not wanting anything to do with the Barcelona factory.

Walther asked, "Did you find out about Hank Morgan, Sam Oliver's assistant? "Who is he?"

"Be careful of him. He is an ex-Marine and known to be violent."

Earlier in the day Krause had talked with Karl Schubach his associate at EuroVinco. They had researched Morgan and discovered he had a troubled past. He had killed three men in an incident with BMP Capital, although Morgan had been cleared of any wrong doing.

Schubach had also informed him that Hank Morgan's actions had brought down BMP Partners and that the lawyer Thomas Bennett was doing everything possible to not be implicated in the affair. So far it looked like Bennett had escaped prosecution.

There was a rumor that Bennett's once handsome face was now extremely disfigured because Hank Morgan had thrown Bennett through a window.

Krause knew Bennett. They had worked together on some buy out deals in the U.S., until Bennett had gotten carried away with this idea of hostile takeovers of startup companies. Bennett approached Krause asking that they work together, but Krause had declined because of some of the larger company buyouts he was working on. Now he realized that his decision had been a good one. It was better to stick with straight forward asset stripping, although his methods might be questionable to some people.

Otto Walther commented, "It sounds like Hank Morgan is more like a bodyguard than an assistant."

"It might be," Krause replied. "Sam Oliver is known to be a cautious man, so maybe that's why Morgan is there. Just be very careful."

They talked for several more minutes where they discussed different scenarios and Otto Walther was given instructions.

Hoerst Krause hung up the phone, satisfied that progress was being made. Occasionally a game of chess can last a long time.

He called Karl Schubach at EuroVinco to give him an update.

CHAPTER 12

They rode with Carme in her small Peugeot while she told them about the Universitat Politècnica de Catalunya, or UPC. It was a technical university with over forty thousand students spread across several campuses in Barcelona and in other cities.

After going into the center of Barcelona she drove down the Diagonal, a main avenue that traverses the city from north-west to south-east, then she pulled off on a street and parked the car.

They got out and she pointed to a group of buildings and said they were part of the north campus of the UPC. The UPC consists of two parts. On the south campus was the school of architecture. On the north campus were the schools of telecommunications and information technology.

As they followed her down the street Hank noticed a motorcycle go by. He thought he had seen it before. In growing up on the streets in Los Angeles one takes a special notice of people and cars. A drive by shooting or any other kind of attack could come from anywhere and you were always on your guard. One noticed drugs being exchanged for money, robbers planning a break-in, prostitutes looking for a mark, and any other happening. Most people from the suburbs were oblivious to these things.

He made a mental note of the motorcycle.

They came to a large grey modern building and Hank saw a small brass plaque next to the door that said, 'Vine Industries Research'.

Carme swiped her identity card through a reader, the door clicked open, and they went inside.

There was a small reception area with no one behind the reception desk.

Carme said, "There are five floors in the building with different kinds of research taking place. On the ground floor and first floor are the training facilities. That's where we take graduates and introduce them to our technologies. Then on the third and forth floor there is research in telecommunications and information technology. On the fifth floor they are doing developing some integrated technologies. That floor has the highest level of security. Not everyone is allowed up there."

"What kind of integrated technology," Sam asked.

She smiled. "You are asking the wrong person. It is very advanced and combines something between computers and radio waves. You can ask them."

Carme led them floor by floor through the training area and then onto the third and forth floors. Sam asked a lot of questions. Carme did her best, but her technical knowledge was limited.

They arrived at the fifth floor and Carme swiped her identity card and a light above the reader turned green. She pulled the door open and said, "Few people are allowed access up here. I have access because I am the recruiter for the company and need to get in here to talk with the head of this department."

Hank scanned the room. It was surprisingly large and in some ways it reminded him of Campbell Labs in Los Angeles. There were people hunkered down over desks and in front of computer monitors, intensely concentrating, almost oblivious to the fact that they had entered the room.

Carme walked over to a man with salt and pepper grey hair and said something to him in Catalan. Then he nodded and walked over to where Sam and Hank stood.

Carme said, "This is Dr. Bascape. He is leading this department."

She introduced Sam and Hank to him.

Dr. Bascape seemed pleased and said, "Mr. Oliver it is a pleasure to meet you. I know you were a friend of Mr. Vine."

"Did you know him?" Sam asked.

"Oh yes. He was here several times and he was the one that mandated the research we are doing? We were devastated to learn that Mr. Vine had been killed."

Sam nodded. "I lost a good friend and I'm hoping we can do our best to keep his excellent company together. Are you able to tell us something about your research?"

"Of course, but not too much. I can tell you in general terms, but we are restricted in our contract to share details to unauthorized people."

"I'd be very thankful if you could give an overview," Sam said. "What is it you are doing?"

Dr. Bascape smiled. "We are attempting to integrate telecommunications with information technology. More specifically, we are developing a new form of wireless transmission much more effective than today's telephone signal. We are using different bands of radio waves to send and receive digital transmissions."

Sam said, "Pete Vine mentioned that to me one time. He said wireless communications from anywhere, or something like that."

"Yes. That's the direction we are moving in. In the future we may be able to achieve transmission distances of hundreds of kilometers, but we are still someway off from that."

They talked for thirty more minutes and Dr. Bascape showed some of the equipment they were developing. It was beyond Hank's knowledge, but he noticed that Sam was up to speed on everything. Hank wished that Robert Campbell could be here, knowing he would enjoy this. They thanked Dr. Bascape and they took the elevator to the ground floor where they left the building.

A motorcycle went by and Hank recognized it as the same one as before.

CHAPTER 13

The hotel was not far away and Carme drove them there. Hank was in the rider's seat in the front and Sam was in the back. Carme and Hank talked about Barcelona and Sam noticed that they seemed at ease with each other.

That gave time Sam time to think about what he had just seen. More than that he wondered why Ramon Mateu had been reluctant to mention the research activities taking place in that building. Mateu had said it was primarily a training center.

Sam now saw that it was much more than that. It gave Sam an uneasy feeling to know that Mateu had been holding back information. Was there something else he was not sharing?

Dr. Bascape's research was indeed advanced and if successful could revolutionize computing as it is done today. It meant that wireless transmission antennas could be positioned at farther distances and mobile devices could pick up signals from just about anywhere.

The applications for this were endless. For instance, TechZip would benefit from this. It was feasible that one antenna could be setup in a warehouse and it could monitor every single piece of inventory all the time. You would not need people walking through the rows holding their handheld scanners.

The financial ramifications were enormous, if it worked.

Sam had already determined that the Sant Cugat factory would make a nice fit with Unipac. It was well run, manufactured good products, and it was making a profit, just what he would have expected from anything that was part of Vine Industries.

But, with the addition of this integrated telecommunications and computing technology, it greatly increased the value of the total operation. Now he understood why Dicio was interested in this.

Dicio's method was to scare away other bidders and then drive down the price of the potential acquisition. Once they did that, they would purchase the asset, break it up, and then sell the pieces to other companies for higher prices. Indeed, the technology in the research lab would obtain a very high price.

Ramon Mateu had not been forthcoming about the research lab and that made Sam wonder if he was working with Dicio.

Sam didn't like the two Dicio men, Hugo Aaron from Madrid and Otto Walther from Frankfurt. During the presentations the previous day they had been condescending to the presenters and carried themselves with a degree of arrogance.

More than that Sam knew what Dicio was capable of doing. Dicio was not well liked in the business world. He needed to be cautious for they were indeed cunning and vicious foes.

One unknown piece of the puzzle was GauLux Holding. Sam couldn't figure out why they were involved in this. While GauLux was run by a flamboyant Frenchman, the company didn't have the same negative reputation as Dicio. Why were they here?

Pierre Dubois had seemed distant, just observing others. Sam considered that Dubois was just going through the motions. Why would GauLux be wasting Dubois' time?

Sam needed more information for he knew that Dicio would do anything possible to achieve their aims. When he got back to the hotel he planned to spend some time on the telephone with Paul Kent and to ask some of their legal staff to investigate Dicio.

The discovery at the research lab was a pleasant surprise, but why had he not been told about the technology?

They got back to their hotel and Carme parked her car in a parking area reserved for guests. As they got out of the car Hank noticed the same motorcycle going by. The rider wore jeans, black boots, a black leather jacket, and a black helmet with a tinted visor. Therefore he could not see the rider's face, but he was certain it was the same motorcycle.

Hank wished he could stop the motorcycle to ask him why they were being followed.

Carme went with them into the hotel lobby. It was late afternoon and she offered to show Sam and Hank around Barcelona.

Sam declined saying that he would appreciate some rest and that he needed to make some telephone calls.

Hank was pleased for the invitation. Since coming to this city they had seen little other than the Placa Catalunya and Las Ramblas. He knew that Barcelona was an exciting city with many things to see and do. And, he found himself attracted to Carme. She was gracious, fun and beautiful. What better way to spend an evening.

He went up to his room, changed from his business suit into a pair of slacks, a sweater and a light jacket, and then he went back to the lobby to meet Carme.

"Where are we going?" he asked.

"I suggest that we see La Sagrada Familia," she answered.

"What's that?"

"A church?

Hank gave her a quizzical look. "I'm not much of a church goer," he stated.

She laughed. "After this, maybe you will be," she stated.

"Okay, let's see." He smiled.

They went outside to the car and Hank scanned up and down the street. He didn't see the motorcycle, but suspected it was around.

* * *

Hugo Aaron and Otto Walther were in a bar near their hotel. It was noisy, full of men drinking beer and wine.

Aaron ordered wine and Walther ordered beer, sticking with their cultural preferences.

Aaron said, "It is unfortunate that they visited the research lab."

"I know," Walther answered. "That makes our negotiation more difficult. Unipac will now see more value in the entire operation and therefore will offer a higher price. We need to scare them away from the deal and then get the price down."

Walther understood Dicio's methods, as he had worked many times with his boss Hoerst Krause on buying companies. Walter knew what was expected. And Krause had given them clear orders on this one.

"What's next?" Aaron asked.

"We have been instructed to destabilize the factory, and likewise to put pressure on Sam Oliver. We want him to walk away from this."

"And how do we do this?"

"The employees at the factory are going through a time of uncertainty. That's good. We can play on that. They will look to their leaders to give reassurance. But without a leader it will destabilize things even more."

"Ramon Mateu?" Aaron asked.

"Yes. He has been cooperative with us because of our, ah… encouragement. Yet it is not certain that he will continue to follow our commands. We should help him take a break from work."

Aaron smiled. "I like it. That idea makes sense. I will instruct our team to take necessary actions."

"It's a start," Walther affirmed.

"What do you think of Hank Morgan? It is still uncertain why he is here with Sam. Oliver." Aaron questioned.

Otto Walther paused for a moment and said, "I agree with you. He seems to be a bodyguard. Look at the size of him. But, why would Sam Oliver have thought to bring one? At the meeting yesterday Morgan hardly said anything. I don't understand why he is here."

"What shall we do with him," Aaron asked.

"If Morgan is removed from the picture, then Sam Oliver will be alone. Then it will be easier to unsettle him and play with his mind. Can our team do something?"

Aaron nodded. "Our man on the motorcycle informed me that Morgan and Carme Cesca-Anglesa are in her car and are going somewhere."

"I don't like it that she took them to the research lab," Walther stated.

"It's not her fault. Ramon Mateu had informed Francina to keep them away from the lab, but Francina had failed to inform Carme."

"Even so, Carme is now too close to Oliver and Morgan,"

"Should we remove her too?" asked Aaron.

"I think so."

"It's a pity. *Ella es muy hermosa.*"

"Don't worry," Walter said. "Once we finalize this deal you will have enough money to buy all the beautiful women in the world."

Aaron reached into his jacket pocket, took out his mobile telephone and called the leader of their team on the ground.

CHAPTER 14

Carme found an empty place to park her car and they walked a block until they came to a small park. The sun had set but there was still plenty of light in the sky.

In front of them stood an immense structure that Hank had a difficult time to describe. It was the strangest building he had ever seen in his life.

"Wow," he said, speaking perfect Californian.

"Yes," Carme laughed. "It is a wow."

"What is it?" Hank asked.

"It is the Basílica i Temple Expiatori de la Sagrada Família. A church"

"Well that explains it all." Hank laughed.

The building was immense, almost indescribable, a series of tall spires that reminded Hank of a child's sand castle on the beach in California. But here there were statues imbedded in the spires.

"They are still building it and hope to have it completed in ten or twenty years," Carme said. "There is still time for us to go inside."

They walked around one side of the cathedral and she bought tickets and they went into the main interior area where Hank saw tall columns supporting a roof. The ceiling resembled something out of a Star Wars movie.

Carme went over to one corner where there was a small statue of Jesus on the cross and she crossed herself. She came back to Hank and said, "The Pope has consecrated this building."

"He has a sense of humor," Hank said.

Carme smirked.

"But what is the history of this place?" Hank asked.

"It was designed by the famous Catalan architect Antonio Gaudi and construction was begun in the early 1880's. So many things happened since then that they lost his original plans, but they try and follow his concept. Anyway, it is a mix of Gothic and Art Nouveau."

"And maybe something else," Hank exclaimed. "This is really cool."

"We call it an expression of the Catalan spirit. Gaudi inspired so many of our Catalan artists like Miro, Picasso and Dali."

Hank had heard of Gaudi, and of course the artists she mentioned. "Well, the Catalans are definitely creative."

"Yes we are, but we are also a sober, hard working people."

"I'm curious to know if you are from Catalonia? I can't help but notice the blue eyes and blond hair," Hank said.

"My name is definitely Catalan. Carme is the Catalan version of the Latin, Carmen, or song. And blue eyes and blond hair are common for many people in Catalonia. For centuries this has been a land invaded and visited by many different people from the Greeks and Romans to the Visigoths that came down from Germany. Perhaps it is from them that we get our features."

"Well, the Visigoths did a good job." Hank said.

Carme blushed and said, "Thank you."

She quickly changed the topic. "On top of this roof they will put the tallest spire, with a cross on the top. It is the spire of our lord and savior Jesus Christ."

"Are you a believer," Hank asked.

"Of course," she answered. "Are you not?"

"Ah… as a teen I lived in a Baptist home." Hank thought of Clyde and Rochelle his foster parents and of their deep belief in God and their influence in his life. "I guess I'm on the fence," he said.

"I will say a special prayer for you," Carme stated.

"Thank you. I need prayers," he said.

They walked around the center of the church shaped like a cross and then a man announced something in Catalan. Hank understood that it was time to leave.

They went outside and began walking back to the car. It had turned dark and the street lights were on.

As they approached the car four heavy set men were walking their way.

Hank eyed them and sensed they were concentrated on him and that there was something hostile. His street sensitivities were now operating in full gear.

Without any warning one of the men pulled out a knife and waved it toward Hank.

"*¿Qué quieres?*" Hank asked.

"*Nada,*" one of them answered.

Hank moved in front of Carme as the men fanned out in front of him.

The man with the knife took a stab toward Hank, but Hank slapped the man's wrist to the side and with one swift movement he stepped close to the man and gave him a right uppercut even harder than the one he had given the pick pocket. The man fell backward onto the ground.

The other three men moved quickly. Two of them jumped at him and he felt a fist glance off his head. For a second he felt a shock in his brain and experienced a flash, but instinct took over and he delivered a hard elbow to the face of the man on his right and then he went for the man who had delivered the blow to his head.

The man must have been a boxer, for he took a boxer's stance. Hank shifted to a wrestler's tactic and went in low to the man's legs, lifted him off the ground and then cracked him hard to the concrete. He kneeled over the man and with one hard blow shattered the man's cheek.

Three men were down and he turned around and saw the forth man standing behind Carme and he had her in a neck lock squeezing the wind out of her.

That meant that the man was stationary so Hank moved quickly and grabbed the mans wrist to try and release the pressure on Carme's neck while at the same time he delivered a driving blow to the man's ribs. Hank thought he felt something crack so he hit the man again. The man let loose of Carme and Hank moved to him and began to hit him again and again in the ribs. The man went down to the ground on all fours, and Hank kicked him again in the ribs and the man went flat, unconscious.

Hank started to kick him again, feeling that latent uncontrollable anger now taking over, but he saw Carme rubbing her neck and he stopped from kicking the man and he went to her.

She began to cry and he brought her close to him, hugged her and said, "Its okay now but we should get out of here."

They got in her car, Hank in the driver's seat, and he drove away. Three men lay still on the sidewalk, whereas the forth was attempting to stand up.

Carme wiped tears from her eyes.

Hank knew it had been a shock for her. He guessed he should be feeling some kind of aftershock, but instead he felt adrenaline and anger rushing through his veins.

He looked in the rear view mirror and saw the motorcycle, so he stopped the car in the middle of the street, got out, and started to run toward the motorcycle.

The motorcyclist saw Hank coming and did a quick U-turn and sped away in the opposite direction.

CHAPTER 15

They sat in a quiet café bar in a residential area of Barcelona. There were few customers and the waiter sat on a chair and was reading a newspaper.

"Do you know who they were?" Hank asked.

"I have no idea. It is so strange," Carme said. "It's been two nights in a row, first with the pick pockets and then with these four men." She took a deep breath.

"Interesting city," he stated.

"No. It's not like that. For sure we have some pick pockets and thieves like in other cities, but the violence of these men is unusual. The Catalan people are different."

"Something strange is going on," he stated.

"The motorcycle. What was that about?" she asked.

"He was following us," Hank said not wanting her to know that the motorcycle had been following them ever since he met Sam Oliver at the Barcelona airport.

They had ordered a small carafe of red wine and a large plate of tapas; dried meat, slices of sausage and a basket of bread on the side. Neither of them was touching the food.

Hank now felt his nerves at work and understood that Carme would be feeling the aftershock. He wondered why all this was happening and he didn't have any answers. He considered that Barcelona might be a dangerous place and that this was a common event in this city, but he didn't think so. Barcelona had a reputation of being a fairly safe place. It certainly wasn't like the neighborhoods where he had grown up.

The strange thing was that the four men didn't seem intent to rob them. They were there to do bodily harm. That meant someone put them up to it because grown up men didn't go around like wild teenagers just looking to do harm to others, for no reason.

His only thought was that this had something to do with the factory, but did that really make sense?

Why would the factory be connected in any way to the pick pockets and to the attack this evening? The scary thing was that one of the men had a knife and it certainly looked like he was going to use it. He wondered how far the man with the knife would have gone and then he remembered that one of the men had Carme in a neck lock and he was squeezing the life out of her.

This was getting dangerous. He needed to update Sam and they needed to be hypercautious from this point on.

He wondered if they shouldn't just discontinue this visit and go back to California. But Hank was stubborn and something in his soul told him to fight this, for indeed fighting was one of the few things he was good at, not that he was proud of it.

Carme put a handkerchief into her purse and said, "I'm shaking."

"It's normal," Hank said. "That was an unexpected aggression. We had a very nice time inside that church and we were walking peacefully down the street. An attack like that rattles the nerves."

"It is a difficult time," Carme said. "We are already nervous in not knowing what will happen to our jobs and to the factory."

"Don't worry. If Sam Oliver is involved you can be sure that he will look out for people. I know. I've been around him for a few months and have seen how he operates. Paul Kent, the CEO of Unipac is exactly the same."

"That's reassuring, but we are not sure that Unipac will end up being the owner. Dicio Partners and GauLux Holding are in the competition and they have the European Union on their side."

"The EU has already given their approval to Unipac, so that shouldn't be a problem. It's Dicio and GauLux who bring complexity to the equation."

"Do you think they have anything to do with what happened tonight?"

"Who knows? Maybe, but we would need to find a connection. If it happens another time I'll take one of those guys and ask him some questions."

"How do you defend yourself like that with so many people?" she asked.

"I was in the U.S. Marines and learned a few things," he said, not telling her that he was a self defense instructor.

"Well you learned well." Carme gave a small smile.

"Just enough," He said.

"And I heard you speak Spanish. I heard you tonight," she said.

"That's another story," Hank stated.

CHAPTER 16

S am Oliver was on the telephone with Paul Kent, the CEO of Unipac. He had given him an update of the events over the past few days, covering the presentations from the previous day and the discovery of the advanced technology in the research lab. He also told him about the pick pocketing event and what Captain Valls, the police officer, had told him about someone hiring the thieves.

"I'd like to know more about Dicio," Sam stated.

"Yes, it seems strange that they came in so late in the game, as well as GauLux Holding. I thought it was a done deal that we were the primary bidder on the factory."

"It was really strange to walk into the factory yesterday and find out they were involved, and even stranger to be in the same room with them all day."

"How was it?" Paul asked.

"Pierre Dubois from GauLux was extremely reserved. The two men from Dicio were something different, quite arrogant."

"From what we know of Dicio it sounds typical, doesn't it?"

"Yes," Sam answered. "They have successfully engineered a long string of hostile takeovers, so it's probably getting to their head."

"What shall we do?" Paul asked.

"I'd like to know more about Dicio, about deals they have done in the past and how they operate. Can you get someone to do some research? I'd suggest someone from our legal team," Sam said.

"I'll do that. When should I call you?"

"Tomorrow morning at seven."

Sam knew there was a nine hour time difference with California and that meant that it was morning over there. Therefore it would give the lawyers all day to do their research. Paul would call him at nine in the evening California time, seven in the morning in Barcelona. Hopefully they would come up with some helpful information on

Dicio, although he wasn't sure what it would be.

Sam figured that if it came to a bidding war Dicio would not be able to match the financial strength of Unipac although Unipac did not currently have huge reserves. The recent acquisition of the Vine Industries operations in North America had weakened the balance sheet. For sure Unipac was still on a solid financial footing, but you can only extend yourself so far before you have to stop. They had not yet reached that point, but Sam knew they needed to be wise.

Sam called room service and ordered a meal to be brought to his room and then he took out a notepad and began to write down his thoughts.

★ ★ ★

Otto Walther put his mobile telephone in his pocket and looked up at Hugo Aaron who sat opposite from him. He had lost count of how many glasses of beer and wine they had consumed.

"We have very bad news," he said.

"Tell me," Aaron said.

"Paco, our man on the motorcycle, just informed me that the four men were unsuccessful in completing their task."

"What?" Aaron exclaimed in surprise. "What happened?"

"They approached our objects as instructed yet something went wrong. It seems that Hank Morgan somehow got the upper hand and he incapacitated them. Two of them are severely injured and the other two have minor injuries."

"That's unbelievable," Aaron paused for a moment and said, "It proves one thing."

"What's that?"

"Hank Morgan has got to be a body guard. For some reason that we don't know, Sam Oliver brought him on this trip. Sam Oliver must have suspected something before he came here. That's got to be it."

"That's a theory, yet we do know that Hank Morgan sold his company and is now working for Unipac."

"Still, how do you explain all of this and what should we do?"

Walther reflected for a moment. "We will continue with our plan to unsettle Sam Oliver and then get him to pull out of the negotiations."

"So what shall we do with Hank Morgan?" Aaron asked.

"I think it would be beneficial if he was removed, but first I'd like to discuss things with Hoerst Krause."

"I agree. We must take Morgan out of the picture. He is too dangerous and is getting in the way of our plans."

CHAPTER 17

The following morning Sam Oliver was unsettled. Paul Kent had called him at seven o'clock as planned and they spoke for half an hour. Now his mind was racing.

He had known about Dicio from things he had read in business magazines, but what Paul had told him seemed almost unreal. Whenever Dicio got involved in a buyout then bad things happened to people. There were instances of people getting into accidents, homes burning down, even people disappearing. Some people had accused Dicio of wrong doing, but nothing was every proven in a court of law, if a legal case even got that far.

Dicio was a company with far reaching influence. With their headquarters in Frankfurt and offices in major cities around Europe, they seemed to have special influence with leading politicians in the European Union. They also had an offices in Washington D.C. and New York and sometimes they made hostile takeovers of companies in the U.S.

And every time they acquired a company it was followed by blatant asset stripping with a slash and burn attitude that left personal destruction in its wake. This had given Dicio a considerable cash reserve for which they could make future acquisitions.

Sam learned that Dicio was run by a set of partners and it was difficult to know exactly who ran the company. Some people pointed to a German by the name of Hoerst Krause, a man who avoided the spotlight. Unipac's legal team suspected that Krause was the brains behind the company. Not much was known about him.

Sam reflected on this. Maybe he had taken Dicio too lightly. Maybe he should just walk away and let them take the factory and the advanced technology at the research lab. But something in Sam could not let this happen. He had made a commitment to save the life work of his friend Pete Vine. Of course Pete and his wife Dora were not around to realize this, but he the least he could do was to preserve Pete's legacy.

Unipac had been successful in purchasing all of the North American pieces of Vine Industries, and while the EU had hindered them from pursuing the European pieces, at least Unipac was given the green light to buy the Barcelona factory.

Sam thought of all the people that worked at the factory. Pete Vine would have wanted the best for those people, and that's exactly how Sam felt about everyone working for Unipac. To have Dicio take over the factory and then break it up and sell it off was unacceptable to Sam. He didn't want one single person to lose their job.

Now was the time to be cautious, yet proactive. The Board of Directors of Vine Industries had hired Wall Street Capital, a large financial institution to manage the divestiture of all of the Vine Industries assets. Wall Street Capital was a financial institution that specialized in Initial Public Offerings, or IPOs, mergers and acquisitions.

Unipac had established a good working relationship with Wall Street Capital through its purchase of the North American assets of Vine Industries.

During their telephone call Sam had asked Paul Kent to call Wall Street Capital and put an offer on the table for the factory. They needed to get the ball rolling. If the past was an example, the buyout could happen quickly. Sam knew that they needed to stay a step ahead of Dicio. The livelihood of many people was at stake.

Sam left his hotel room, took the elevator downstairs and saw Hank Morgan waiting in the reception area. He noticed a look of concern in Hank's eyes.

"Good morning," Sam said. "Did you have a good evening?"

"Something happened," Hank stated.

Sam motioned for Hank to go over to a quiet area of the reception area and then asked, "Tell me about it."

Hank said, "We were attacked when walking back to Carme's car, near la Sagrada Familia, the Gaudi church."

Sam asked, "What do you mean by attacked?"

Hank recounted the events of the previous evening up until the point where he and Carme had left the café bar. She had driven home and he had taken a taxi back to the hotel.

"What do you think?" Sam asked.

"I think it was more than a coincidence," Hank stated. "They were purposely there to harm us. I'm wondering if there is a connection with the factory."

"I'm coming to the same conclusion," Sam said, especially in light of the information Paul Kent had given him this morning. "My assumption is that Dicio has something to do with this, but for now we don't have a proven connection. Let's try and discover something today."

"What's the plan?" Hank asked.

"We are meeting with Ramon Mateu at nine o'clock at the factory. He doesn't know it, but Paul Kent will be calling Wall Street Capital today to make an offer for the factory. He will be calling them in the middle of the night in California, hoping to speak with them at eight thirty in the morning East Coast time. There is a six hour time difference between New York City and Barcelona. So, the call will be made at two thirty Central European Time. Wall Street Capital has nothing personal in this game and they have been instructed by the Vine Industries board to take any reasonable offer within given parameters. We are putting a premium on our offer because of what we discovered yesterday at the research lab. We should have an answer from them by this afternoon, or by the latest tomorrow. Unless Dicio or GauLux Holding makes a counteroffer, then the factory will go to Unipac. If a counteroffer is made, then we may get into a bidding war."

"I hope it moves fast," Hank affirmed.

"Me too, but we have to be prepared for any eventuality. And most of all we need to be extremely cautious around Dicio."

CHAPTER 18

They arrived at the factory and went into the reception area and asked for Ramon Mateu. A few minutes later Francina Bissom walked toward them taking short quick steps. Hank sensed she seemed nervous.

"Mr. Oliver and Mr. Morgan, could you please come to my conference room next to my office," she said.

Hank noticed that she had addressed them formally, rather than by their first names.

"What is it?" Sam asked.

"Please come. I'll tell you in a minute," she said.

They followed her down the hallway leading through the administrative wing of the building and then walked toward her office. They passed Carme's office and Hank saw Carme behind her desk. He waved at her and smiled. She nodded but without a smile, her eyebrows raised.

Hank wondered if he had done anything to upset her. Indeed the attack the previous night with the four men had been shocking.

Next to Francina's office was a conference room. They entered it. It was small and had solid walls on all four sides. There was a large round table in the middle with eight chairs around it. Hank suspected that confidential meetings took place in this room.

They sat down and Francina said, "Something terrible has happened."

"What is it?" Sam asked.

"Ramon was in a car accident." She took a deep breath.

"Is he okay?" Sam asked.

"No. The accident happened this morning when he was on his way to work. He is in very serious condition and is now on the operating table at the hospital."

"What injuries did he suffer?" Sam asked.

"It's not clear. They said he has multiple fractures and perhaps a punctured lung. We will find out more today."

"What are the circumstances of the accident?"

"Ramon was driving through an intersection near his house and a large truck crashed into the side of his car. That is all I know." She paused. "The driver of the truck is not found." She looked down. "This can't be happening. It will unsettle everyone and we are already nervous enough. It is not good."

"Who takes over when Ramon isn't here?" Sam asked.

"It depends. He often delegates responsibility to others when he goes on trips or is on holiday, but Ramon is the leader."

Hank didn't know a lot about management, other than what he learned through his MBA studies, but he knew that Latin people put a lot of importance on their leaders. Indeed, this would be another unsettling event for people in the factory.

"How will you handle this?" Hank asked.

"To handle it?" she replied.

"To inform the employees and to encourage them."

"I don't know. I'm not even sure I'm the right one to do it."

Hank thought about it for a moment and concluded that an announcement had to be made as soon as possible to avoid untrue rumors from spreading.. Maybe the news was already out, so the employees had to be given reassurance. He asked, "Who knows about this accident?"

"The hospital called me about ten minutes before I saw you. I was with Carme, so she knows. Other than that I don't know."

"Then I suggest that quick action is needed," Hank said.

Sam nodded. "Francina, I agree." He turned to Hank and asked, "What do you suggest?"

Hank was surprised that Sam asked for his ideas. Surely Sam had the experience to deal with this.

"It seems to me you should start by getting all the managers together and inform them. As the Human Resources Manager you would be seen as the person to take the lead on this. And then work how they should inform their people. Then you and Carme should drop everything else you are doing and make yourselves available throughout the day. The emergency meeting with the managers should happen as soon as possible."

"Can Sam come?" She asked.

Sam said, "No, I think its best that I'm not there. We don't want to confuse the acquisition with this accident. If we are around it will only heighten the tension. You will have to do it on your own. Is that okay?"

"Yes, I understand." She stood up. "Carme and I need to call all the managers."

CHAPTER 19

Sam and Hank stayed in the conference room and waited for Francina. Sam reflected on what he had just heard and indeed it was troubling. It was another unsettling event and he didn't know how much more of this he could handle. Maybe it was best to step away and gain some perspective. But, the offer would be submitted to Wall Street Capital in a few hours and they needed to be ready for any contingency.

After a few minutes the door opened and the two men from Dicio entered, Hugo Aaron and Otto Walther.

Aaron and Walther had a look of surprise on their faces.

Walther said, "Ah, Mr. Oliver. We didn't expect you. We thought that Miss Bissom was here."

"She's at a meeting," Sam said.

"Do you know where?"

"I'm not sure. She will be coming back."

"Then may we wait," Walther said, "unless you are discussing something private? In fact, it may give us an opportunity to discuss things with you on a gentlemanly basis."

Sam motioned for them to sit down and Walther and Aaron took up places on the opposite side of the table from him and Hank.

Otto Walther looked at Sam and said, "We know that our companies are in a competition to purchase this factory, but perhaps we might discuss the process so we all may have a clearer idea where we stand. My associate and I are curious to know how your evaluation is coming, and whether Unipac is interested in the factory."

"We are considering it," Sam said not telling them about the offer to be submitted to Wall Street Capital. "What is the interest of Dicio Partners in this factory?"

Hugo Aaron glanced at Walther and turned back to Sam. "It is an operation that has a perfect fit with our overall portfolio of assets."

"And what is your portfolio of assets?" Sam asked.

"We are a diversified conglomerate that is building up a set of core competencies," Aaron said.

"I'm not so sure," Sam stated.

"What do you mean?" Walther asked.

"From what I know of Dicio, your core competency is asset stripping and the destruction of successful companies. I don't see a diversified conglomerate, other than a set of assets being broken up and sold to the highest bidder."

"Well, you haven't done your research," Walther stated, his voice hard and accusing.

Aaron stared across the table, his jaw tight eyes narrow. Hank stared back at him, not blinking, relaxed, a slight smile on his face, a look he had perfected on the streets of Los Angeles.

Aaron turned away.

Sam said, "You better believe we have done our research. Dicio leaves destruction on everything it touches."

"I'm sorry you see it that way," Walther responded, "but perhaps you have no knowledge of business in Europe and I can see that Unipac should limit itself to North America. This factory is a bad fit for you."

"We'll see," Sam said.

"I don't think it's profitable to speak with you," Walther stated.

"Probably not," Sam said. "You definitely will get no profit from Unipac."

"Then I think our friendly conversation is finished." Walther stated.

"I didn't expect a 'friendly' conversation," Sam said.

"Do you know where we can find Miss Bissom?" Aaron asked.

"She's busy," Hank said, his eyes still fixed on Hugo Aaron.

Walther said, "For your information, Dicio is prepared to take the next step in purchasing this factory. I think it is only fair to inform the opposition. Of course you may want to consider backing out. As you may be aware, our European politicians are reluctant to allow an American company to take over a European operation."

"It's already owned by an American based company, Vine Industries." Sam said.

"Well, now is time to shift the ownership to Europe," Walther countered, "so you may just save face and walk away. If you don't, then things could escalate."

"Is that a threat?"

"Oh no. We don't work like that, but things do happen. Life is full of unexpected events. Consider what happened to Ramon Mateu."

"How do you know about that?" Sam asked.

Walther smiled. "Things happen, even if you have a bodyguard." He looked over at Hank.

Walther and Aaron got up from their seats and walked out of the room.

CHAPTER 20

"That was strange," Hank said. He felt like he had been in some kind of street confrontation when one gang meets another, where threats and intimidations are made, only this had taken place in a business conference room.

"Yes. During all my years of doing business I've been in some tough negotiations and even some where threats were made, but they were made on a commercial level, like, 'I'm going to run you out of business,' and things like that. But, I don't think I ever had an encounter like that," Sam said.

"It was an attempt at intimidation."

"More than that. I see it as a physical threat."

Hank realized it had gotten to his nerves. Sure he could face people on the street and be as cold as ice, but on the streets a physical response was always possible, and he was good at that. But here it was threats going across a table in a commercial environment and he didn't know how to respond.

Hank was glad that Sam was there. Sam had been so composed and straight forward. He laid the facts on the table. And when the intimidations were made, Sam didn't back down. Hank admired that.

From what just happened, Hank realized that Sam had a backbone of steel. And Sam wasn't like those at Dicio who destroy and break down. Hank knew that Sam's intentions were to redeem and build up. More than anything he saw that Sam wanted to preserve Pete Vine's company and in doing so he had the best interests of the employees at heart.

One thing that bothered Hank was what they said about a 'bodyguard'. Is that how Aaron and Walther perceived him? Indeed, he had taken the pick pockets out of action, and he had disarmed the attackers from the previous night. Did they know about that? Maybe that's why these Walther and Aaron had come to that 'bodyguard' conclusion..

They said, "things happen, even if you have a bodyguard". That was an indirect threat.

They definitely knew about Ramon Mateu's accident. How did they find out? Hank assumed that Francina was the only one informed about the accident, and she knew about it shortly before he and Sam had entered the factory. So, the news was recent.

Hank concluded that Aaron and Mateu knew about the accident because they had something to do with it. They had shown no compassion when they mentioned the accident. In fact, they used it to make a threat at Sam.

It was becoming clear in Hank's mind that Dicio was a dangerous company..

He wondered what Sam was thinking. More than that, what should be their plan of action?

Most of all he was determined to be very cautious and to do his best to look out for Sam.

★ ★ ★

The door opened and Francina and Carme walked into the room. Hank looked at Carme and saw that her eyes were red. The events from last night and this morning were taking their toll.

"How did it go," Sam asked.

"They were shocked," Francina said. "We worked out how to inform everyone in the factory."

"How do you think the news will be received," Sam asked.

"Who knows? This will be a difficult day and people will be nervous."

"They need you, both of you," Sam said. "I'd suggest that you spend most of the day being visible, in the coffee areas and in the cafeteria. People need time to process this and they will need your support."

Francina sat down in one of chairs. "What about the long term? What if Ramon Mateu doesn't live, or if he is not able to return? Who will take over his job? There's no one left at Vine Industries that's making management decisions, and we don't know who will end of owning the factory. We want it to be Unipac, but that is uncertain. The acquisition may take a long time and we feel lost."

"I very much understand how you feel," Sam said. "Hopefully things will move faster than you expect. Just be patient. Today you are seen as the leader because you broke the news and worked with the managers on the communication plan. At some point a solution will emerge, but I'd suggest that you take on a public role, at least for today."

"I'm not the right person for the long-term," Francina stated.

"Don't worry," Sam said. "We can help you find a solution. In the mean time we've got some challenges on our hands. The men from Dicio may want to see you and that could get complicated."

CHAPTER 21

Sam was very troubled by the meeting with the Dicio men and he wondered what Dicio's next move would be. Today Unipac would be submitting an offer to Wall Street Capital and he expected to hear from Paul Kent by the end of the day. Hopefully they would get some clarity on where they stood. But for now he figured that his presence at the factory might be a distraction.

"I think we should get out of here," Sam said. "Our presence in the factory could confuse things. People need to process the shock of what happened to Ramon Mateu. They don't need to be thinking about the future of the factory and their jobs. If we are here it will just add to the complexity and I don't think there is much we can do."

Sam knew that Hugo Aaron and Otto Walther had left the building ten minutes before. Pierre Dubois from GauLux Holding had showed up and tried to set up a meeting with the factory's Accounting Manager. In light of Ramon Mateu's accident, the meeting was postponed. Dubois was wandering around the factory somewhere.

Sam didn't consider GauLux to be a threat although he couldn't figure out why Dubois was here. All Dubois had said was that GauLux was interested in purchasing the factory but without any further information than that.

Sam went with Hank to one of the coffee areas to find Francina and saw Carme talking with some people. Sam told Carme that they would be leaving and he gave her his business card so that they could call him if he was needed.

Sam noticed Hank eyes looking at Carme and suspected that the young man was attracted to her. He didn't blame him. She was tall, slim, had thick blond hair down to her shoulders and had sparkling blue eyes. She had a great personality and related well with people. Today her eyes were drawn and she appeared tired, as though she had missed sleep.

He knew that the attack during the previous night must have been extremely unsettling for Carme and he was sorry that she had been pulled into this.

Sam thought back to the first time he had met Hank. It was at a trade show in San Jose. There, Hank had an assistant by the name of Sharlee, a very bright and lively young woman. Sam suspected that Hank was attracted to Sharlee, but Hank recently shared that Sharlee had gotten a job in Los Angeles and she now had a boy friend.

Sam sensed that Hank was sad because of this. Hank had also shared that he had not been too successful with women. He claimed it was because of his upbringing, and that he always ended up driving women away.

Sam considered this. He saw potential in the young man. He was smart and he showed leadership qualities. Hank was definitely a man of action. Seeing him deal with the pick pockets was a confirmation of that. The fact that Hank had completed an MBA and had pursued an entrepreneurial idea also said something about him.

This morning in the conference room Hank had shown leadership abilities in helping Francina with an action plan for dealing with the news of Ramon Mateu. That was a pleasant observation.

Indeed there was something about the young man and Sam wanted to help him.

Margaret always remarked that Sam put people before anything else, and he knew she was right. Hank was on his radar screen.

They walked to the reception area and ordered a taxi.

Hank asked, "Where do we go from here?"

"I think we should just go into Barcelona and walk around and talk, just to get away and reflect a bit. I'd also like to call, Captain Valls the policeman we spoke with the other night. Maybe he can help us get an update on Ramon Mateu's accident."

The taxi came, they got in, and it sped away toward the city.

Hank forgot to turn around and look, but in the distance behind them the taxi was being followed by a motorcycle.

* * *

Karl Schubach the director of the Frankfurt office of EuroVinco received a telephone call from Hoerst Krause who gave him an update on the progress being made in Barcelona. Schubach was Krause's silent partner in the acquisition of the Barcelona factory.

Schubach reflected on the information he had been given and then responded, "So, the pressure on Sam Oliver is being turned up. That is good. Unipac should be out of the picture before Dicio makes an offer. That way we can drive the price down."

"We are not sure Unipac will back out. Sam Oliver seems quite determined."

"I would have expected that. One doesn't become a billionaire by allowing people to run over you," Schubach knew that because he had a plan to become a billionaire, and Sam Oliver's assets were part of that plan.

"We need to get him to back off. Do you have any suggestions?" Krause asked.

"Why not start with the bodyguard, if that's what he is. What was his name?"

"Hank Morgan," Krause replied.

"Yes. By removing him, I'm sure it will destabilize Oliver."

"Then I will inform my men in Barcelona to pursue that track."

"Good. Please keep me informed," Schubach said.

Karl Schubach thought about the events in Barcelona. Perhaps they had been foolish to compete with Unipac on the acquisition of the factory. He knew a lot about Sam Oliver, having built up a considerable dossier of Sam Oliver's history. He knew where he lived, his interests, his religious convictions, and just about everything personal about the man. And of course he had a record of every business transaction Sam Oliver had made.

The Sant Cugat factory was only a minor play. Schubach knew that Unipac did not have a strong presence in Europe and the company needed more business from Europe in order to grow. No matter what happened Unipac would need to expand in the European market.

There were several ways to do this. First, they could expand through sales of their existing products. Second it could be through acquisitions of successful European companies. A merger was a third alternative, and that is the one that Schubach preferred, and EuroVinco would be perceived as an ideal partner. It would give EuroVinco access to Unipac's core decision body. This was a method that Schubach felt comfortable with. It was a method he and his EuroVinco partners had perfected in the past.

In light of this, whether Unipac purchased the Sant Cugat factory, or not, it didn't really matter. His plan would work one way or the other. Hoerst Krause didn't know this.

Fundamentally, Karl Schubach didn't like Hoerst Krause. Krause's form of business didn't suit Schubach. Krause's method was to acquire assets and destroy them, while extruding a profit out of the pieces. Schubach's method was different. It was to acquire assets and build an empire. He knew that when were at the top of a large corporation you gained recognition from others and you acquired power. Schubach desired great financial wealth, but even more than that he wanted power.

He knew that he had some similarities with Krause. They had no reservations about using any method necessary to get what they wanted. Rules and morality didn't mean anything and they both used the political and economic system for their advantage. For that Schubach was wary of Krause, as loyalties are nothing more than an alignment of people to achieve one's interest. And because of this he knew that Krause would turn on him for any reason. Hoerst Krause was a cunning man. Therefore Karl Schubach knew that he needed to be even more cunning.

He knew that Hoerst Krause was a chess player and they now had a chess game in front of them. Schubach chuckled. The only thing was that Krause thought the game was one thing, whereas the real game was being played on a much bigger board.

So, if Dicio didn't end up with the factory it didn't matter.

Karl Schubach dialed a telephone number to speak with one of his EuroVinco partners, Jacques Gaubert. They needed to discuss the next move.

CHAPTER 22

Sam asked the taxi driver to let them out at the Placa Catalunya. It was lunch time and they decided to find a restaurant where they could spend time to review their plans. Sam had not yet told Hank that Unipac was going to put in an offer for the factory in two hours time.

Most restaurants in Barcelona start serving lunch at one in the afternoon, but in the area of Las Ramblas there were many tourists, and the restaurants were more flexible with their opening hours.

They found a tapas bar, went in and ordered several plates of potatoes, calamari, sliced ham and some baked zucchinis in tomato sauce.

Sam said, "I didn't have time to tell you, but Paul Kent will be calling Wall Street Capital in a couple of hours to make an offer for the factory."

Hank responded, "That's fast."

"Yes, but I felt we needed to get out in front of the pack. If we let Dicio continue to do their thing it could get very messy. It would be best to bring this to a conclusion."

"How long will it take for Wall Street Capital to make a decision?" Hank asked.

"Our other deals with them went through very fast. The Vine Industries Board of Directors gave them carte blanche to accept any reasonable offer. They want to avoid endless bidding wars. Their objective is to cash in and move on."

"It sounds like the Board is in a hurry," Hank commented.

"For sure and that's something I don't understand. During the past year there was a turnover of people on the Vine Industries board. Pete wanted to reflect the international nature of the company and he brought in people from Asia and Europe. They thought differently than the board members from the past. Of course Pete controlled the company and the board eventually followed his lead. But, with Pete out of the picture it gave the newcomers the freedom to do anything they wanted. And selling the company was what they decided. I think it was an absolutely terrible decision."

"But Unipac obtained much of Vine Industries," Hank stated.

"I can't say we are not pleased to have Vine Industries as part of Unipac, but the events and circumstances by which it happened were unthinkable."

Sam paused, his fingers moving over his fork. "You know, Pete and I talked about merging our two companies although we never came around to doing it. We were just two guys who spent a lifetime building up our respective businesses and I guess we wanted them to maintain their uniqueness. That's fair. But now its happening and I wish I could be happier about it."

"I understand," Hank said.

They finished their meal and Sam pulled out the business card of Captain Valls. Sam took out his cell phone and dialed the number on the card. The policeman answered and Sam asked if they could have a meeting, and Captain Valls agreed. He was based in the Placa Catalunya Police Office, which was close by. Sam was given directions.

Sam paid the bill and they got up to leave when his cell phone rang. He answered.

It was Carme. She said, "I have bad news to pass on to you."

"What is it?" Sam asked.

"It's Ramon. He didn't make it. He died in intensive care after the operation."

CHAPTER 23

Hank and Sam walked quietly. The police station was just off the Placa Catalunya. They went into the police station and walked up to a reception desk. A row of seats was along one wall where people were waiting.

Sam wasn't sure that Captain Valls could help, but he felt it wouldn't hurt to have the police on their side.

Sam nodded to the man in uniform behind the desk and said, "Excuse me, but do you speak English."

"Yes," the man said.

"We have an appointment with Captain Valls.

"Just a moment," the desk officer said. He lifted a telephone tapped a couple of numbers and spoke something in Catalan, then turned to them. "He will be here soon."

Two minutes later Captain Valls appeared from a hallway on one side of the front desk. He walked up to Sam and Hank and said, "How can I assist you?"

"I'm wondering if you could help us gain some information. It concerns the pick pocketing incident from the other night, we think."

Captain Valls looked puzzled. "Pick pocketing is a fairly common crime in Barcelona, with all the tourists who come here. In your case it was unusual that a victim defended himself when Mr. Morgan incapacitated the thieves. Between us I'm pleased that thief was taken off the streets. And yesterday I saw a known criminal with his hand in a cast. I spoke with him but could not get any information."

Sam said, "We believe there is something related to the pick pocketing incident. Yesterday morning you said that the thief in the hospital told you someone had hired them to take my wallet. We think it is more serious than a simple theft."

Captain Valls said, "You are a known man Mr. Oliver, the founder of a large corporation. Perhaps someone thought you might be carrying a lot of money."

Sam saw that Captain Valls had done his homework. "It is more than that. Someone was killed this morning and we think the people behind the theft had something to do with it."

Captain Valls' eyebrows rose. He said, "Please come with me."

They followed him down a passageway and into Captain Valls' office. The desk had several piles of papers.

They sat down in empty chairs and the police official took his chair behind the desk. "Tell me," he said.

"What we say is speculation," Sam said. Then he told the police official about the attack on Hank and Carme near La Sagrada Familia, about Ramon Mateu's car crash.

"We would like to know if the police have found out anything about Ramon's Mateu's car crash. Did they find the driver of the truck?"

Captain Valls' eyes rolled up as he paused for a moment and then he said, "This is very unusual. Is it possible that so many events can be connected?"

"We are not sure. We are just trying to put some pieces together," Sam said.

"I can try and find out something," Captain Valls said. "But it will take time to know who is handling the case as it is in another district. We also have a number of different kinds of police in Barcelona.

While the responsibility lines are clear between us, at least on paper, sometimes things overlap."

"Different types of police?" Hank asked.

"Yes. The Barcelona's system of law and order currently relies on more than one type of police force. We are the Mossos d'Esquadra, something particular to Barcelona. We have been around since the early 18th century and our main function is to protect the freedom and security of citizens in the city. We investigate and deal with crime in the city including robberies and pick pocketing. Then there is the Cuerpo Nacional de Policia, the Guardia Civil, and the Guardia Urbana. And there is also the Policia Portuaria. They look out for the ports. I will need to determine who is handling the accident with Mr. Mateu. I will do that and then connect you to the proper authority."

"That would be most helpful," Sam said.

They thanked Captain Valls and left the police station.

Hank said, "The number of police forces in Spain sounds complicated. Do you think he will be able to help us?

"I hope so," Sam said. "It just doesn't feel like Ramon Mateu's accident was an accident."

Hank said, "I think you're right. It makes me think of something that happened during our first day in the factory."

"What's that," Sam asked.

"Hugo Aaron was putting some pressure on Ramon." Then Hank told of the conversation he had overheard in the hallway.

"It's all starting to tie together, isn't it," Sam stated.

"So, what do we do from here?"

"Perhaps we should have stayed at the factory, but I'm glad we had the discussion with Captain Valls. In another hour I should be hearing from Paul Kent. Wall Street Capital will probably not make an immediate decision based on their telephone conversation, but maybe Paul will at least have some indication of what they are thinking. Let's head back to the factory to see if we can help Francina and Carme."

They found a taxi and ordered it to take them to Sant Cugat. The taxi went onto a major avenue and then took an express way that eventually led west.

Hank turned around and looked out the back window and then turned to Sam.

"There's something else I didn't tell you about," Hank said.

"What's that?"

"Ever since you arrived at the Barcelona airport we've been followed."

CHAPTER 24

H oerst Krause was on the telephone with Otto Walter. Walther had just given an update on the events of the morning."

Krause said, "The demise of Ramon Mateu is a pity, but it was one of the risks involved. In fact, it works in our favor. Anything we can do to heighten the tension in the factory will help." Krause was extremely pleased, as the death of Mateu meant absolutely nothing to him. This was the best possible outcome and he was delighted that it was moving in the right direction.

"What should we do next," Walter asked.

"Who is running the factory?"

"For the moment no one has been assigned. Francina Bissom is temporarily seen as the leader, as everyone is going to her for information."

"You need to get to her. If she is unsettled, then everyone else will feel it, like a ripple effect."

"What should we tell her?"

"Use your creativity," Krause commanded. "Make her uncertain of herself. Threaten her if necessary. Do anything to reduce the value of that factory."

"Okay, we will head back there immediately," Walther said. "And what about Sam Oliver and his bodyguard?"

"Eliminate the bodyguard. If that doesn't cause Oliver to walk away, then it will necessitate more drastic measures. In fact, if both of them were taken out of the picture it would create serious reservations in the minds of the decision makers in Unipac. Just remember that there is hidden value in this factory and it will give Dicio considerable profits if we can sell them off. We need to buy low and sell high."

"We are working on a plan for the bodyguard. We could include Sam Oliver."

"Well, good. Now make it happen," Krause commanded. Then he hung up the telephone.

★ ★ ★

Before they walked into the factory Sam called Paul Kent. It was seven o'clock in the morning in California.

After three rings Paul answered. "What time is it?"

"Three o'clock in the afternoon in Barcelona. Seven o'clock in the morning in California."

"I was just trying to get in a few minutes of sleep. It was a very short night."

"I'm sorry to bother you but what was the feedback from Wall Street Capital?" Hank asked.

"It went well. They were expecting to hear from us and our offer was within their parameters. They just need to check with someone at Vine Industries and then it should be a done deal."

"Do you think the EU will backtrack on their decision to let us take the factory?"

"I don't see how they would change their mind. They restricted us from going after the major Vine Industries assets in Europe, but they needed to allow something to go through. Otherwise it would have opened a trade war with the U.S. This is a token offer that will satisfy members of our government. And in the broad scope of things this factory is not a big purchase. From here it should be smooth sailing."

"Did Wall Street Capital give any indication of how long it would take them to confirm the sale?"

"The decision should be made today or tomorrow. Then we can make the announcement."

"That would be good," Sam stated. "The factory here is going through a difficult time. I think it would help settle things down if we could make an announcement. The people here are nervous about their future and we need to help them."

"What's going on over there?" Paul asked.

Sam gave him an update about the pick pocketing event, the attack on Hank, and the death of Ramon Mateu.

"It sounds like Dicio is a nasty bunch of thieves."

"If it's them, and we think it is," Sam stated.

"What can I do?" Paul asked.

"I think it would be helpful if you were here to make the announcement, if the sale goes through. That would be a very nice gesture for the people here in the factory."

Paul said, "I'll get on a flight the minute I hear from Wall Street Capital."

"Thanks," Sam said.

Paul paused for a moment then said, "In the mean time, be careful."

★ ★ ★

Hank and Sam went straight to Francina's office. She wasn't there. Then they looked for Carme and found her talking with people in a coffee area.

She was speaking to them in Catalan. Hank noticed that their faces were drawn and they were quiet.

When they walked into the coffee area Hank noticed that everyone turned to look at Sam. Hank understood that Sam represented Unipac, the company that might end up owning the factory.

Carme nodded, forcing a smile.

Hank was happy to see her.

"How's it going," Sam asked her.

"It is a difficult day. We grieve to know what happened to Ramon."

"I know," Sam said. "Hank and I are extremely saddened to hear the news."

Someone in the group of people spoke up and said, "Mr. Oliver, is Unipac going to buy the factory?"

Sam turned to the man who asked the question.

Hank knew that whatever Sam said it would spread like wildfire, perhaps getting twisted as the information moved from person to person.

Sam said, "This is a fine operation and Hank Morgan and I have been extremely pleased to find such a well run business. We have met so many capable and wonderful people. Of course an operation like this would be a welcome addition into the Unipac family."

"So, you will buy the factory?"

Sam smiled. "I'd love to give you more detailed information,. You must understand that a decision like this involves discussions and negotiations. But we are positive and want things to move in a good direction."

"Who will be the manager of the factory?" the man asked.

Sam looked at Hank and then back at the man. "Perhaps Hank Morgan could tell you something."

Hank took a slight step back. "I'm not sure what to say."

"Tell them about TechZip and how this factory could be a good fit."

"Ah... sure," Hank said. He looked at the small group of people. A few more people had joined it. "Well, when I was studying at the University of California at Los Angeles I began to develop this idea. One of the finest technical minds in California helped me with it. It's revolutionary and will change the way inventory is tracked and that will bring benefits to every kind of manufacturing and retail company. I sold my company to Unipac and now I'm helping with the integration. One thing Sam and I have seen that the Sant Cugat factory has complementary competencies. That's one of the reasons we are favorable. But even without that, we feel you have an exceptional future. All of you can be proud of what you have created."

Hank wasn't sure he had said the right thing, but he noticed a small smile on Sam's face. He looked at the man who asked the question and saw a degree of relief in his eyes. Hank realized he had not given a specific answer to the man's questions, but something better. He had encouraged them. That's what was needed most in the midst of this difficult news.

Sam said, "Look, we hope to get more information to you in the next couple of days, which will be communicated by Francina and Carme. Please be patient. And again, we deeply feel the tragedy of what happened to Ramon Mateu."

The group of people waited for a minute and Sam turned to the coffee machine and pushed a button and a minute later he had a cup of coffee in his hand. Then Hank did the same.

People walked away.

Carme looked at Sam and Hank and said, "Thank you. This has been a most difficult day."

"Yes, I totally understand," Sam said. "Where is Francina?"

"I think she is meeting with Hugo Aaron and Otto Walther."

CHAPTER 25

Sam saw Francina walk to the coffee area, her eyes fixed in a gaze at the floor. As she got closer it seemed that Francina had been crying.

Her shoulders jerked a bit when she noticed them.

Sam said, "Hello. How are you doing?"

"Not well," she stated.

"Maybe we might go talk somewhere," he said.

"Perhaps it might help," she replied.

Sam said to Hank, "Could I ask you to spend some time with Carme, if that's okay?"

Hank nodded.

Sam understood that Francina was unsettled and it would be better if they could talk confidentially without Hank and Carme being there. He knew that the death of Ramon Mateu was a traumatic event, but there might be something else working on Francina's emotions and he needed to find out.

He walked away with Francina, leaving Hank and Carme next to the coffee machine.

They went to the conference room next to Francina's office and sat down next to the large circular table.

"Please tell me how you are feeling," he said.

"Terrible," she answered. "This is one of the worst days of my life."

"I understand," he empathized.

They sat for a moment in silence and then Sam asked, "Do you have more information on the accident?"

Francina shook her head back and forth.

"I think you met with the men from Dicio," Sam stated. "How did that go?"

Francina shook her head again and she started to cry, sobbing, taking deep breaths, tears coming from her eyes. She didn't have a tissue so wiped the tears with the back of her hand.

Finally she stopped, took a deep breath and said, "They are not nice men."

Sam waited a moment. "Why do you say that?"

"I shouldn't say it. In fact, I shouldn't say anything."

"What did they want from you?"

She looked down at her hands which were now folded in front of her, resting on the table. "They want me to spread information."

"What information?"

"They want me to tell things that are not true?"

"Like what?"

"I am to tell everyone that they are going to lose their jobs if the factory is purchased by Unipac."

"What would that accomplish?" Sam asked.

"It would turn the workers against Unipac resulting in industrial action. The Catalonia government would get involved, as well as the Spanish government in Madrid. And, they have connections with the EU in Brussels. It would slow down the purchase of the factory. They said that Unipac needs to back out of the competition."

"Unipac would never fire all the workers," Sam stated "The factory represents a thriving business and it would become stronger if it were part of Unipac. Why would they want you to spread these rumors?"

"It's obvious. They will do anything to own the factory. Otto Walther said the factory would be better off if Dicio owns it."

"Why did they come to you?" Sam asked. He thought he already knew the answer.

"I'm the Human Resources Manager and have a big influence on the personnel."

"Did they make any threats to you?" he asked.

Francina looked at her hands. One thumb was rubbing the other. "I can't say."

"So they did threaten you?"

She nodded.

"I'm assuming they mentioned Ramon's accident," Sam stated.

She nodded.

"Did they threaten your family?"

Francina took a deep breath and tears came from her eyes. "Sam, I have two young teenagers and a husband. I can't let anything happen to them."

"These guys are evil to the core," Sam stated. He thought for a moment then asked, "Would it be a solution if you and your family took a trip to a safe place somewhere, for a few days or a week or two?"

Francina was quiet and Sam considered that she might be thinking through the alternatives. She said, "The factory needs me."

"Yes it does, but your family needs you even more so. If you are gone for a period of time the factory will survive but getting you away from here to a safe place seems to be the best option. Would you consider it?"

She thought for a moment and said, Yes, can you help?"

"I can. Do you think you could leave on a trip this evening? He asked."

"This evening?"

"Yes. You saw what happened to Ramon. We must be very cautious."

"My family can be ready," she said.

"Let me make a telephone call," he said.

Sam took out his cell phone and made a call to California and spoke with Paul Kent. He gave him a quick update and asked him to do something.

Sam and Francina waited and in a few minutes Paul called back.

Paul said, "It's being arranged. It will be at the Girona airport. A taxi will pick them up at their house at seven o'clock. Call me back when you get her address."

"Thanks," Sam touched the stop button and he put the phone back in his jacket pocket.

"Francina, you must go home at your regular time as though everything is normal. A taxi will pick up you and your family at seven o'clock. Don't take any bags, as we want to make it look like you are going somewhere local. The taxi will take you to the Girona airport. Do you all have passports?"

"Yes," she said.

"Good. A private jet will be waiting for you at the airport and we will take care of you and your family from there. Unipac has some facilities where you will be safe."

"And where is that," she asked.

"In Florida."

CHAPTER 26

Sam and Francina emerged from the conference room and Francina headed for her office. Sam went in the direction of the coffee area to give Hank an update.

Sam felt anger over what was going on. He had never in all his business dealings encountered something like this. He knew he was a stubborn man with a great resolve, but this was wearing on his emotions and he was afraid it would affect his judgment.

In the past there were times he had competed with cutthroat businessmen who tried everything to squeeze every penny out of you in their negotiations, even using criminal methods to achieve their goals. But in his mind Dicio represented evil of the worse kind. He knew he couldn't directly pin the attacks on Dicio, but everything pointed to them.

Sam wondered if this was common for companies in Europe. He had been to Europe quite a few times during his career and he had learned that business was a bit different here where a lot more weight was put on business connections and political relationships. Sure they exist in the U.S. but not to the same extent as over here.

He questioned if other companies in Europe used dirty methods like this to gain an advantage? If this practice was pervasive over here, then he felt like walking away and just letting Europe sink into oblivion.

He rounded a corner and saw Hank and Carme talking with some people. Hank saw him and Sam nodded for Hank to come over.

When Hank got to him, Sam said, "I think we should stay in the factory until closing time."

"What's going on?" Hank asked.

"It seems the Dicio men are making threats to Francina. I can't go into all the details here, but Paul Kent and I came up with a plan to move her out of harm's way. We just need to stay here until she leaves the factory. That should be in another hour. I'll tell you about it later."

"Okay, what should we do?"

"Just hang around the coffee machine and talk with people," Sam said.

★ ★ ★

Hank wondered what Sam and Paul Kent had planned for Francina, but more than that he wondered what threats Dicio was making. Hank didn't like Otto Walther and Hugo Aaron and he had to hold back his anger. He knew that anger was an uncontrollable emotional reaction that he carried, a genie in a bottle. Once it was let out then it was capable of doing anything. He felt he was getting better at managing it, but there were times in his past where his violent reaction to things had terrified him.

Selling TechZip and then joining in with Unipac had been good for him. It had given him a new purpose and he was beginning to feel confident about himself. Yet these attacks and Ramon's death aggravated his anger problem and he knew where that might lead. This had to stop. He didn't want to get back into that emotional state he had constantly lived in as a teenager.

Now that his life was on a new path, he knew he needed to deal differently with things in life. He thought of Rochelle his foster mother. She said that if he went to God he could be helped. She was a psychologist and she relied heavily on spiritual things. Hank knew that his anger had been a barrier to God, and at the end of the day wasn't he just blaming God for all that had happened in his life. But, should he be thanking God for the good things?

Hank was determined to do things in a new way. Anyway, it wasn't his role to bring justice to Dicio. If Dicio was responsible for the aggressions, then he needed to let others deal with it. Unipac had made the offer to Wall Street Capital and things would work out in their own way in their own time. He decided the best thing he could do was to stay with Sam in the coffee area and just try and encourage people. He found that he enjoyed doing that.

Hank took a coffee, his sixth for the day and he put it on a counter fixed to a wall. Sam was with him and people stopped to talk with them during their coffee breaks. Carme had gone back to her office to take care of some paperwork.

The main questions asked by people had to do with the future of the factory. Sam gave the same answer as before. Discussions were in progress and they hoped the result would be positive.

Sam used these encounters to ask people their names and what they did in the factory.

Hank began to copy Sam and do the same. At one point he heard two men speaking Spanish. Most people in the factory spoke Catalan, but other languages were spoken. He knew that most of the Catalan people also spoke Spanish.

Hank spoke to the men in Spanish and they smiled in surprise. It resulted in a long conversation as they asked him where he learned the language. He shared that it was almost a mother tongue in that it was the principle language he used in growing up in California.

Others heard Hank speaking Spanish and before long a small crowd of people were around him. One person said they liked his Mexican or Central American accent. Hank knew that his Spanish was different than that spoken in Spain. The Hispanics in Los Angeles used different expressions and the accent was different, yet he perfectly understood Castilian-Spanish. It was comparable to British and American people speaking with each other.

Hank saw Sam smiling at him.

After an hour at the coffee area, Sam and Hank headed for Francina's office. She was putting on her jacket.

They entered her office and Sam said, "Just remember to keep everything as usual. Then the taxi will arrive at your house and will take you away. It will be okay."

She nodded and left the office.

Hank wondered if indeed everything would be okay. It was almost like nothing had been 'okay' since they had arrived, and it was very sad what had happened to Ramon Mateu. He hoped the same thing would not happen to Francina.

They waited several minutes and Sam said, "I think we can go now."

They went to the reception area and ordered a taxi and in a few minutes one arrived.

They got into the back seat of the taxi and Sam gave the name of their hotel.

Hank looked over and saw a motorcycle parked in one of the visitor parking places. A dark helmet was attached to the motorcycle with a flexible lock. The motorcycle seemed similar, like the one that had been following them.

Then Hank saw movement as a man in jeans and a black leather jacket approached the taxi and he opened the front door on the rider's side and he got in. He turned toward the back seat. In his hand was a gun and he pointed it at Sam.

The man said, "Mr. Bodyguard, if you make any movement your boss here will get a bullet in his heart."

CHAPTER 27

Hank guessed that the gun was a .38 special, not as powerful as a .45, but more than enough to instantly kill a man.

His initial thought was to reach forward and grab the gun, but it was pointed at Sam's chest and the man's finger on the trigger seemed steady and sure. He couldn't take the risk of going for the gun because if anything went wrong, Sam would be dead in a split second.

Hank told himself to wait for the right opportunity, if it would ever come.

The man with the gun spoke Spanish with the driver and told him to go.

The taxi driver said, "*Si, Paco.*"

The taxi went out onto the main road and instead of turning toward Barcelona it went in the opposite direction and then into an older section of the town of Sant Cugat. They came to a small industrial zone and the taxi went down a narrow street where all the buildings were made of brick. He turned into a small courtyard and then drove through an opening into what appeared to be an old warehouse, and then the driver stopped the motor.

Paco got out, pointing the gun at Hank. He stepped away from the car and then said in Spanish accented English, "Get out, on this side."

They got out on Hank's side of car then Paco said, "Lean against the wall over there." He pointed with one hand to the wall on the opposite side from the entrance.

The taxi driver went to the doors of the entrance and shut them which cut out some of the light coming into the building. It was the end of the day and the room was dark, with some light coming in from a few broken windows at the top of one of the walls.

Hank looked around. The warehouse was not particularly large. It had a dirt floor and the only way out was through the main entrance, which was now shut. The warehouse was empty except for the car. Hank was looking for an escape route or something to hide behind. There was nothing.

Hank felt stupid that they had gotten themselves into this situation. Had he been a bit more attentive, perhaps he would have seen the motorcycle without the rider. Even as the man had approached the taxi Hank could have done something. And perhaps he should have gone for the gun in the taxi no matter what the risk. Now the risk was even greater.

Paco stood some distance away from them, pointing the gun at Hank, occasionally shifting it toward Sam, but most of the time on Hank.

Hank figured that at some point Paco would have to drop the gun to his side, as the human body can't hold an extended weight for an indefinite amount of time, even if it is not that heavy.

At the same time, Paco was far enough away to raise the gun and fire, even if Hank had a running start.

The driver was leaning against the front of the car. He had a knife in one hand with a blade about eight inches long. He was using the tip of the knife to clean his fingernails.

"What do we do now?" Hank asked.

"We wait," Paco said.

★ ★ ★

Sam's legs were getting tired. They had been standing stationary for at least fifteen minutes. Even though he was able to lean against the wall he felt he needed to move his muscles, but every time he moved the man pointed the gun at him.

Sam had travelled around the world for many years and this was the first time he had ever had a gun pointed at him. He knew they were in danger and he felt fear. He knew what happened to Ramon Mateu and the gun in the man's hand was an ominous sign. He knew this could be the end of his life.

But what he felt bad about was Hank. This was a young man who had grown up in a difficult environment and he had fought his way out of it. The young man had tremendous potential and Sam regretted that his life could end this day. Because of that he regretted that he had even asked Hank to come on this trip with him.

As far as what happens after life, Sam was a believer. He had grown up with parents that believed in God and his mother had taught him from the Bible. Sam didn't believe that life ended when you took your last breath; that it was just 'lights out', as though the switch was turned off. Every person had a soul consisting of a unique personality and a living spirit that extended beyond physical life.

For this Sam had a reassurance, but still to face one's death was a nerve racking experience that hit the inner core of his being. He thought of the unpredictability of life. How many people get up in the morning thinking this could be their last day on earth?

He knew he needed to do something, anything, to try and avoid their fate. But at that moment it seemed bleak.

Sam said, "What do you want?"

"Silence," Paco said. By now the gun was hanging low in front of him and he was supporting it with two hands.

There was some noise and then a knock on the door. Paco motioned to the driver who then walked quickly over to the door and opened it. In walked Otto Walther and Hugo Aaron.

Otto Walther had a smirk on his face. They walked over and stood next to Paco. Paco raised the gun and pointed it at Sam.

"What do you want with us? Why are you doing this?" Sam asked.

Walther smiled. "Isn't it obvious? We want the factory and the technology at the research lab."

"Fair enough," Sam stated, "but why do you go through all this, the aggressions, Ramon Mateu's accident, and now this?"

"You are a perceptive man. You made the assumption that we were behind the pick pocketing and the other things. You are known as a man with much insight. This has proven to be true." Walther chuckled, his voice deep.

"It doesn't take great insight to add one and one together," Sam exclaimed.

"Even so, we may not have needed to resort to all of that if you had not brought your bodyguard."

"He's not a bodyguard," Sam stated. "Hank is here to help me with the evaluation, and that's it, period."

"He is quite an assistant. We believe you brought him as protection. He severely injured several of the people we hired and they were tough men." Walter turned toward Paco and said, "Keep the gun pointed at the bodyguard. He is dangerous."

"Your methods are evil," Sam said.

"Evil is in the mind of the beholder," Walther said. "Maybe your methods are evil to us?"

"You don't go around killing people to achieve business ends."

"Who says?" Walther asked.

"Is that how things are done in Europe?" Sam asked.

"I don't understand the problem," Walther stated. "Now we need to ask you some questions."

"Like what?"

"Where do you stand on making an offer for the Sant Cugat factory?"

"What do you mean?" Sam asked.

"Did you decide to make an offer?"

"That's confidential to Unipac."

Walther pointed at Hank. Then he turned to Paco and said, "Shoot him."

"Wait, stop," Sam pleaded.

Walther held up his hand in front of Paco. He said, "Now you better stop playing games and answer our questions. Have you decided to make an offer?"

"We are thinking of it," Sam said.

Walther smiled. "We know it is more than that. Our superiors at the Dicio office in Frankfurt contacted Wall Street Capital. It looks like there is an offer on the table."

"I guess so," said Sam.

"Then it has to be taken off the table," Walther stated.

"The offer is already in process. I can't do anything."

"Oh, Mr. Oliver. Do you think I am asking you to do something? We are beyond that. At this point things require something dramatic, so repulsive that Paul Kent, and the other decision makers in Unipac will not want anything to do with the factory. If they find your bullet filled body it will have a psychological effect."

Otto Walther turned to Hugo Aaron and Aaron nodded.

Aaron looked at Paco and said, "*Tírales!*"

CHAPTER 28

The moment Hank heard the command to 'shoot them' he sprang into action.

He had stood there long enough and the anger inside him had reached a breaking point. He was now beyond reason. He understood that they had been brought here for one purpose. It wasn't to negotiate. It wasn't to discuss or share information. It was to kill Sam and him.

The violent death of Sam Oliver would send shock waves through the business world. The psychological impact would significantly drive down the share price of Unipac. And then Unipac's management team would need to go into a defensive mode and they would have to protect the financial health of the company. It would be extremely likely that the offer to purchase of the Sant Cugat factory would be taken off the table. Then Dicio could name their price.

Hank hated them. When he heard the word 'tírales', the caged aggression in him was let loose and he charged forward like a line backer.

Hank's action caught Paco by surprise and it took a moment for him to steady his gun and he pulled the trigger but the shot was off center.

Hank felt something hit him in on his right side, but he kept moving forward straight into Paco knocking him backwards onto his ground. Hank was now on top of him, the gun wedged between them and Hank had his left hand on Paco's wrist and he forced the barrel of the gun into Paco's stomach and with his right hand he squeezed Paco's finger and a shot went into Paco's chest.

Hank stood up as fast as he could but it was painful and he saw his shirt turning read.

The driver was now headed toward Hank with the knife in his hand. Hank felt dizzy, but using one of the movements he perfected during his time in the U.S. Marines, he deflected the driver's hand, and then with a powerful elbow strike to the temple, the driver went to the ground.

Hank turned and saw that Sam had gone after Hugo Aaron and they were wrestling on the ground. Sam was behind Aaron and had his legs wrapped around Aaron's waist and one arm was around his neck and Sam was attempting to get him into a neck lock. Aaron was trying to squirm away.

Then Hank saw that Otto Walther was reaching for the gun that was now lying next to Paco. Walther grabbed it, raised it and fired a shot, but it went wide and Hank moved fast and with his left hand knocked Walther's arm so that the gun was now pointed off to the side and then he bunched the knuckles of his right hand into a karate fist and made a hard strike directly into Walther's neck, directly into his larynx.

Hank felt cartilage break and Walther dropped the gun and brought both hands to his neck as he fell to his knees. Walther began to breathe with a gurgling sound and in a few seconds he was on his side coughing, attempting to take in air. Walther tried to speak but couldn't as blood dribbled from his mouth and he coughed several more times and then he stopped breathing.

Sam and Hugo Aaron were still wrestling. Hank picked up the gun walked over and smashed it to the side of Aaron's head, and Hugo Aaron went limp.

Hank went down on his knees a deep throbbing pain now pervading through his right side. He touched his ribs with his left hand and saw that his hand was covered in blood.

Sam was rising up and Hank handed him the gun and said, "You better call Captain Valls."

After that Hank fell forward and everything went black.

CHAPTER 29

Ten days later Hank walked out of the hospital. It had been touch and go for a few days. The bullet had broken a rib and then angled off into his liver and that caused extensive internal bleeding. The doctors had worked rapidly to repair the damage and then it was a process of wait and see.

Hank slowly recovered but he needed to stay in the hospital to allow time for his body to heal. Captain Valls and another police officer from Sant Cugat had come to see him, to get a statement of the events that had taken place.

Sam Oliver visited him every day and as Hank began to recover they talked about what had happened in the warehouse and the status of the buyout. Unipac's offer had been accepted and Wall Street Capital had announced the acquisition. They also discussed the future of the factory, how to advance TechZip, and the leadership in the factory. Sam had made a proposition.

What had pleased Hank the most was that Carme had visited him every day.

Hank wasn't able to attend Ramon Mateu's funeral. He learned that it was a cheerless affair, knowing that the accident had been engineered by Dicio.

As Hank walked through the automatic door of the hospital, he slowed when he stepped outside, feeling the warm sun on his face. In some ways it felt like the warmth of California. He looked around and saw a black luxury car parked in front of the hospital and he headed for it. His ribs were still sore, but now it was much easier to breath.

A driver in a dark business suit came out and opened the door for him and Hank moved onto the back seat.

Twenty minutes later the car stopped in front of the main entrance of the Sant Cugat factory. Hank went inside and made his way to Francina's conference room. There was no one there so he took a chair and waited.

Four minutes later Sam Oliver and Paul Kent walked in. They were smiling. Sam carried two coffees and he handed one to Hank.

"Black, right?" Sam asked.

Hank smiled. "Yes."

"You're looking good, all things considering," Sam said.

"Much better." Hank paused for a moment and asked, "When is Francina coming back?"

"In a few days," Sam said.

In actual fact it was unnecessary that Francina and her family needed to continue on the private jet to Florida. They could have turned around and come back, but once in the air Sam just let it go. Francina and her family were now enjoying a holiday in Florida thanks to Unipac.

"Do you have any news of Dicio?" Hank asked.

"The taxi driver told what he knew. He was part of the same gang that tried stealing my wallet, and the ones who attacked you near la Sagrada Familia. He said he was hired by Hugo Aaron."

Hank remembered how the driver had come after him with the knife. "And Hugo Aaron?"

"The police have a long list of charges against him including the murder of Ramon Mateu, although they are not sure that one will stick. They still don't know who was driving the truck that crashed into Ramon's car. Aaron made a plea deal by pointing the blame at someone in the Dicio headquarters in Frankfurt."

"In Frankfurt?"

"Yes. It seems that one of the directors in that office was orchestrating everything, at least from what Aaron is claiming. The German police are looking for the director but he can't be found. They think he fled to Asia somewhere."

"They sound like an evil bunch of people," Hank stated.

Sam was still. "I guess there are companies out there that will do anything to break the rules. We are fortunate that things worked out in our favor. And I'm most grateful for what you did in that warehouse."

Hank tried not to think about what happened. He had killed two men in self defense. In searching his soul he thought he may have felt a slight sense of regret. But his sense of justice told him they got what they reserved. He knew he didn't react to things like most people.

Hank thought of Sam's reaction in the warehouse and how he had jumped on Hugo Aaron." He said, "You didn't do so bad yourself in the warehouse. I thought I was watching Mixed Martial Arts when I saw you taking down Aaron."

Sam smiled. "He was getting away from me. Luckily you stopped him in his tracks." He paused. "All things considered, I think that Pete Vine would be pleased that this factory is now part of Unipac rather than being broken up and sold to the highest bidder."

Hank nodded.

Paul Kent took a sip of his coffee and then set it on the table. "Are you guys ready?" he asked.

Sam nodded.

Hank asked, "Are you sure you want to do this?"

Paul said, "Absolutely."

"Is Carme here today?" Hank asked.

Sam smiled. "She's there with all the others."

* * *

Sam Oliver was pleased that things turned out well in the end. In fact he realized that he was feeling mixed emotions, anger over what Dicio had done, yet he also experienced elation that the factory was now in good hands.

They walked into one corner of the factory and up on a raised platform that had been quickly constructed. Over eight hundred people had gathered to officially hear the announcement from Paul Kent, the CEO of Unipac.

Paul walked forward and spoke into a microphone. He thanked everyone for the hard work they were doing and then he got on to the topic everyone wanted to hear. The Sant Cugat factory was now officially a part of Unipac and no jobs that would be cut.

In fact, there were plans to move an exciting new technology to the factory, an advanced inventory tracking system called TechZip. Engineers from Unipac's labs in Silicon Valley would be working closely with Dr. Bascape and his lab in Barcelona.

Paul said, "Now I'd like to introduce you to person who will be interim manager of the factory as we manage the transition." He turned and looked behind him and then back at the audience. "Hank Morgan."

An applause was given.

Paul gave a brief statement of Hank's background how he had his own company that he sold to Unipac, and how Hank would be leading the integration of TechZip into Sant Cugat. He would be taking on the role of Manager of the factory.

Hank smiled and walked to the microphone and said a few words in English and then he switched to Spanish. He thanked Paul and said he was looking forward to get to know more people, and how he was confident in the future of the factory.

Sam looked out across the room. It was filled with smiles. He noticed that the biggest smile was on Carme Cesca-Anglesa. Sam wondered if Hank Morgan had now found his soul mate.

Sam reflected on the events over the past couple of weeks. Indeed it had been a roller coaster ride. The experience with Dicio had been a sickening experience, but he was content that things worked out in the end.

During his hospital visits with Hank he had discussed the future of the factory and Sam knew they needed someone to replace Ramon Mateu. Sam had appointed many mangers in Unipac and he saw all the right capabilities in Hank. Hank was a leader. He got on well with people, although he had a tough side, to say the least. Hank had an MBA from an excellent school and he had taken the initiative to start his own company.

Sure he was throwing Hank into the deep end by appointing him as the manager of the factory. They had agreed it would be on an interim basis, and then they would see how things went from there. There was already a good management team in place and these managers knew what they were doing. They just needed encouragement and a listening ear. And they needed a vision for the future. TechZip would be part of that.

Sam had confidence that the young man would make it.

There were still some pieces of the puzzle that Sam couldn't figure out. He knew little of the man in the Dicio Frankfurt office who supposedly was behind the aggressions.

And, Sam still could not figure out why GauLux had been there. Pierre Dubois had hardly spoken a word with them and then he just disappeared from one day to the next. It was very strange.

He thought to himself that sometimes you don't need to know everything and some things in life just remained a mystery.

All things considered he was extremely pleased that the factory was part of Unipac and things would go well from here. It turned out to be a satisfactory ending and he hoped it would provide a stepping stone for the company into Europe.

At the same time he knew that Europe was a complex place with many different languages and cultures. Each country represented unique market conditions. Unipac didn't have the competencies to fully capitalize on the potential in Europe. He knew they needed to gain those competencies, but the Sant Cugat factory was a first step and a good beginning.

EPILOGUE

Karl Schubach was thrilled how things were going. He called his counterpart, the Frenchman Jacques Gaubert based in Nice, France.

"Hello Jacques. Did you hear the news about Unipac."

"Yes," Jacques answered. "Things are progressing. Pierre Dubois gave me and an update."

"He did a good job, didn't he?"

"Indeed."

Schubach knew that Dubois was planted there as an observer, to see that things stayed on track with Dicio and with Unipac. He said, "You need to give him a bonus."

Gaubert paused. "When this venture has a successful conclusion then we will reward him."

"Undeniably." Schubach stated.

"And what about Hoerst Krause, do you have any news of him?" Gaubert asked.

"He is missing. An acquaintance told me he went for a long deep swim in the Rhine River."

"Excellent. We could not afford to have any link from Dicio to EuroVinco, no matter how circumstantial it might be."

"He's gone. Now we can move forward," Schubach stated.

"What's our next move?"

"Unipac now has a foot into Europe, but they need a stronger presence."

"And we can help them,' Jacques responded.

"Yes. We are an ideal partner. I think that Mr. Oliver will particularly like the fact that EuroVinco is holding some of the European pieces of Vine Industries. We can make an attractive offer to him."

"Then let's start to work on it. We need to decide who will approach him."

"Let's continue to monitor him for a while," Schubach stated. "Do you know how the detective in California is progressing?"

"He has planted microphones in Oliver's office and car. I'm getting frustrated that he has not put microphones in his house."

"We should replace the detective if he cannot deliver."

"I agree," Gaubert said. "From this point on we need to know everything that Sam Oliver says and thinks, even in the privacy of his own bedroom. It will be critical to the success of our project."

"And, we also agree that the tactic remains the same?" Schubach asked.

"For sure, we will do the same thing with Unipac that we did with Vine Industries. It should be easier as we now have improved our competencies."

Schubach laughed and thought to himself that the game was progressing. The beautiful thing was that Unipac didn't even know the game was in play. The EuroVinco pieces were now strategically placed and the only possible outcome was conquest.

AUTHOR'S NOTE

We see the world in different ways. From my house in the Costa Brava I look out at the Mediterranean Sea. Just to the north is France. Beyond my view to the east is Italy and to the south is North Africa. And around the rim of the Mediterranean is a mix of countries with different histories going back to the times of the Phoenicians, the ancient Greeks, the Romans, and the Crusaders.

From this, traditions have emerged, each one holding to a diverse set of values and beliefs. The fact is that we all have a worldview, a paradigm — a theory of how the world should be. We live in cultures formed by complex networks of social systems and institutions. They hand us our beliefs, and we accept those beliefs, often without questioning their origins and validity. Yet, our beliefs have a large part in forming our destiny. They establish boundaries for our lives, and we make our choices within the context of those boundaries. In fact, we could say that our destiny is determined when we consciously or unconsciously chose to live by a worldview.

But what happens when our worldview does not have an adequate answer to the reality we experience? And what happens when 'fate' takes us beyond our boundaries and comfort zones?

These are the questions I was reflecting on when I started the Blue Fate series. In *Buyout* it is the simple story of a younger man and an older man joining together to overcome an unknown foe. Each man has a different history and set of experiences as they engage in a life and death mystery in a foreign place. What they are not aware of is that a sinister force is at play. While they may think that the story is finished, in fact it is not. Isn't that how it can be in our lives where the end of one event is actually the beginning of the next?

Could it be in life that we practice our daily routines without awareness that there is something bigger at play that will impact our destiny? That's the door that was opened in *Buyout*, and then expanded in the next novel, *Dropout* (Blue Fate 3).

In *Dropout* the complexity grows. A young business professional loses everything, his job, his family and his identity, so he drops out and ends up in a village in Spain. But even though he attempts to flee from his pain, his previous life comes back to haunt him in a very real way. This book is also the introduction of an unusual predicament that is opened in *Squeeze* (Blue Fate 4). This will present a dilemma and I'm guessing it will be controversial to some readers. It would be interesting to know your feelings about the right solution for the main characters. Even more, what would you do if you were in their situation?

Cass Tell
Costa Brava, Spain

Your opinion is important to me!

I hope you enjoyed my book and I'd love to receive your feedback. As the book is still fresh in your mind, please leave some comments or a review on any of the following websites:

Amazon — www.amazon.com
Barnes & Noble — www.barnesandnoble.com
Goodreads — www.goodreads.com

And I invite you to visit my website www.casstell.com to find out more details about all books in the Blue Fate series and my other books.

Thank you!

www.ingramcontent.com/pod-product-compliance
Lightning Source LLC
Chambersburg PA
CBHW050426110726
47899CB00008B/2867